The
PUMPKIN
WAR.

The
PUMPKIN
WAR

Cathleen Young

A Yearling Book

All rights reserved. Published in the United States by Yearling, an imprint of
Random House Children's Books, a division of Penguin Random House LLC,
New York. Originally published in hardcover in the United States by Wendy Lamb
Books, an imprint of Random House Children's Books, a division of
Penguin Random House LLC, New York, in 2019.

Yearling and the jumping horse design are registered trademarks of
Penguin Random House LLC.

Visit us on the Web! rhcbooks.com

Educators and librarians, for a variety of teaching tools, visit us at
RHTeachersLibrarians.com

The Library of Congress has cataloged the hardcover edition of this work as follows:
Names: Young, Cathleen, author.
Title: The pumpkin war / Cathleen Young.
Description: First edition. | New York : Wendy Lamb Books, an imprint of Random
House Children's Books, [2019] | Summary: Twelve-year-old Billie enjoys summer on
Wisconsin's Madeline Island, where she harvests honey, mucks llama stalls, and grows a
giant pumpkin, determined to reclaim her title in the annual pumpkin race. |
Identifiers: LCCN 2018005490 (print) | LCCN 2018013438 (ebook) |
ISBN 978-1-5247-6735-8 (ebook) | ISBN 978-1-5247-6733-4 (trade) |
ISBN 978-1-5247-6734-1 (lib. bdg.)
Subjects: | CYAC: Farm life—Wisconsin—Fiction. | Family life—Wisconsin—Fiction. |
Friendship—Fiction. | Pumpkins—Fiction. | Racing—Fiction. | Islands—Fiction. |
Wisconsin—Fiction.
Classification: LCC PZ7.1.Y743 (ebook) | LCC PZ7.1.Y743 Pum 2019 (print) |
DDC [Fic]—dc23

ISBN 978-1-5247-6736-5 (pbk.)

Printed in the United States of America
10 9 8 7 6 5 4 3 2 1
First Yearling Edition 2020

$$7 \times 10^{27}$$

That's a number. It means seven billion billion billion. It's the number of atoms in a human body. If you wrote it out, it would be a 7 followed by 27 zeroes.

I dedicate this book to 3 people: 2 precious daughters, Shaelee Sean DeCarolis and Gemma JoLee DeCarolis, and 1 wonderful husband, Patrick DeCarolis.

When I see all of you, when I talk to any of you, when I think of each of you, every atom in my body spins extra fast with happiness and gratitude and disbelief at the miracle of my family. Because of you, my universe is filled with love and laughter and happiness.

Every. Single. Day.

JUNE

❧ 1 ❧

I watched Sam through my binoculars as he planted his pumpkin seedlings. He looked like a two-legged bug I could squash with my thumb.

I climbed higher through a web of tangled branches and emerald-green leaves smeared with sunlight, my binoculars swinging from a braided lanyard around my neck.

My head popped into open sky.

I could see my whole world from up here. Our house looked like a wooden bird that had crashed into the hillside. My dad built it with his own hands before I was born. He says our house is "in harmony with nature." I say it's weird to have a closet hacked from brownstone and a tiny trickle of a stream cutting through the middle of our kitchen during the rainy season.

Up the hill from my house, at the end of a skinny dirt footpath, I spotted my beehives, a row of white wooden boxes stacked like suitcases.

I love my bees. They turn the world into a taste.

When I stick my finger into a fresh comb bursting with honey, I can taste the globe mallows that tickle my neck when my little sister and I lie sprawled on our backs behind the barn, eating sticky jelly beans from my secret stash, and I can smell the purple lupine that explodes across the fields around my house after a spring thunderstorm. I swear I can even feel the cool breeze hitting the brittlebush in the heat of summer.

Sam says that's impossible, that it's just my overactive imagination at work.

What does he know.

I could see my half-built tree house stuck in a towering pine tree and our gray barn slouched next to the feed shed. Our water tank looked like a fat red Tootsie Roll stuck in the middle of the meadow that rolls down from our farm to Chequamegon Bay.

Pronounced *she-wah-me-gan*.

The bay used to be called *Zhaagawaamikong*. It was named by the Ojibwe, who lived here first until we stole their land. I guess I shouldn't say *we*, since

I'm half Ojibwe from my mom's side. My dad is Irish. When I look in the mirror, I see his red hair and green eyes.

The wind kicked up, and whitecaps skittered across the bay. I raised my binoculars and scanned the horizon until I spotted my dad's fishing boat, her bow riding low with his haul of whitefish. He named his boat *Niinimooshe* for my mom, to honor her heritage. *Niinimooshe* means "sweetheart" in Ojibwe.

My mom thinks that's romantic. If she spent as much time on that stinky boat as I did, she might not think so.

I swung my binoculars back toward land and found Sam, still planting his seedlings. All of a sudden he looked up and smiled in my direction. I ducked into the leaves as a prickly heat crawled up my neck and across my face.

Sam used to be my best friend, and he'd like to be my best friend again, but that's never going to happen after what he did last summer.

That night, we had tofu for dinner. Even if you try to drown it in sesame sauce, it still tastes like tofu.

We used to eat meat. Teriyaki steak. Swedish meatballs. Polish sausage. Those were the good old days.

Marylee ruined everything a year ago when she turned five. That's when my little sister put two and two together and realized the steak on her plate used to be alive.

Now she won't touch meat. She won't even look at it. And there's no talking her into it. Believe me, we've all tried. It turns into a lot of yelling (my dad) and crying (my sister) and pleading (my mom) and more yelling (me), and by then no one wants to eat anything anyway.

So we eat a lot of tofu. Mom calls it a "perfect protein," but if you go by taste, it's far from perfect.

"The baby kept me up all night," Mom said, shoveling chunks of buttery baked potato into her mouth.

"How?" Marylee asked. "He's not even born yet."

"He likes to kick."

My mom was so big, she had to sit a mile back from the kitchen table and rest her plate on her belly.

"Can't you make him stop?" Marylee asked.

"Baby's the boss," Mom sighed. "In a few more weeks, your new brother will be right here with us."

While Mom stuffed a piece of not-so-perfect protein into her mouth, my sister dropped her broccoli on the floor and squished it through the heating vent under her chair. She might be a vegetarian, but even she has her limits.

"Good news, Billie," my dad said, his elbows resting on the edge of the kitchen table, which was a slab of granite that grew out of the floor like a giant mushroom with a shaved top. "You can plant your pumpkin seedlings tomorrow."

I stared at him. "What about the frost warning?"

"False alarm," he said with a shrug.

"You could've told me," I grumbled.

"I just did."

"She's just mad because Sam got his seedlings in before her," Marylee piped up, sucking on a green bean like it was a straw.

Almost every kid on Madeline Island grows a giant pumpkin to compete in the annual Madeline Island Pumpkin Race. You start your seedlings in the spring and the pumpkins grow big and round over the summer. In the fall you hack off the top of your biggest one, scrape out the slimy guts, line it with itchy burlap, haul the hollowed-out pumpkin down to the lake, jump inside, and race it across the bay using a kayak paddle.

Last year, just as I was about to blast across the

finish line, Sam sideswiped my pumpkin, breaking it into raggedy chunks.

When he threw a look over his shoulder and saw me bobbing in the water, he looked guilty.

He'd cheated, and he knew it. It's against the rules to ram another racer's pumpkin.

Afterward, he flat-out denied it. He said my pumpkin cratered because of all the rain that spring, that my pumpkin was too waterlogged to hold together.

The judges hadn't seen what happened, so it was his word against mine.

That was bad enough, but then I kept losing to him all through sixth grade.

At the all-school spelling bee, I got *hubris* wrong and he got *escarpment* right. Then, at the science fair, Ms. Bagshaw was *very* impressed with his acid test to tell minerals apart and not so impressed with my comparison of the different respiration rates in goldfish versus humans.

"I'm gonna win the race this year," I declared.

My mom looked up from her plate.

"Life isn't about winning, Billie."

I didn't say anything. Because it is about winning, and everyone knows it. Even grown-ups know that.

That's why they don't cheer when you lose.

2

The next day Sam's rooster woke me up. Some kids think a rooster is the same as a turkey. I wish Sam's rooster would turn into a tom, which *is* a turkey, and go to freezer camp while he waits for his turn to be Thanksgiving dinner.

I wiped the sleep from my eyes. "You awake?" I asked, peering down at my sister from the top bunk.

Marylee's eyes popped open. "I am now."

I slid down the ladder to the floor and dug around in my closet for my favorite cutoffs. They were stuffed behind the old telescope Sam bought at the flea market last summer when he was obsessed with cosmology. I thought cosmology was the department where my mom bought her lipstick. Not even close. Cosmology is about how the universe began and where it's going.

When Sam found out the universe is actually expanding, he wanted to see it with his own eyes, so he got the telescope. We saw cloud bands on Jupiter and rings around Saturn, but we never saw the universe expand.

Mostly we just stargazed.

We'd lie on the grass and stare up at the night sky. The lineup was always changing, depending on the season, so it was like a never-ending light show.

Now Marylee and I slid out of our pajamas, yanked on shorts and T-shirts, slithered into our flip-flops, and snuck down the hall. My mom was still asleep, lying flat on her back, the sheet stretched tight across her belly. She was imitating a giant white sand dune that got lost on its way to the desert.

A plate of freshly baked cinnamon rolls was waiting on the kitchen counter. They were covered with fat wiggly lines of frosting. Think white caterpillars, only you don't want to lick a caterpillar.

My dad always makes us breakfast before he goes out on the lake to fish. Sometimes he bakes squash biscuits where you can't taste the squash, or bran muffins that don't taste like sawdust, or he makes zucchini pancakes that are bright green but still taste like regular pancakes.

My dad can make anything or fix anything or build anything. My mom says he has magic in his hands, which sounds silly, but I guess that's the kind of thing you say when you love someone.

I carried the rolls out to Cami and her little sister, Turtles, who were already waiting on our back porch. Cami and Turtles live across the road on their apple farm. Their mom and dad also raise llamas. People buy llamas as cute yard pets, until they discover their cute yard pet will spit at you when you try and teach him tricks. And llama spit isn't really spit. It's vomit. They can shoot it at you from ten feet away. When people try to bring the llamas back, they find out there are no exceptions to the "no return" policy.

It can get loud over there, which is why Cami and Turtles like hanging out at our house.

Cami has hair the color of fresh-cut straw, and hazel eyes that sometimes pretend to be green like mine. She's obsessed with learning all the words in the English language; she says there are about two hundred thousand. She told me she's going to learn five words a day until she meets her goal.

When she said that, I did the math.

Let's say she lives to be ninety years old. She's twelve, like me, so that leaves seventy-eight more years made

11

up of 365 days a year. And 78 x 365 = 28,470 days. If you multiply 28,470 days by 5 words a day, you get 142,350 words. I didn't want Cami to give up on her dream, so I didn't mention the fact that she'd need to learn seven words a day for the rest of her life to meet her goal.

Cami loves words, but I love numbers. Which is why I love math. Math is black-and-white. The answer is right, or it's wrong. That's why I'm going to be a mathematician when I grow up.

Turtles is six, with hair the color of chestnuts, like Marylee's. Her real name is Hannah, but everyone calls her Turtles because she never goes anywhere without Hector, her pet turtle. Ever since she heard that sea turtles were becoming extinct, she's been afraid Hector will become extinct even though he's not a sea turtle. He's a red-eared slider. I don't know how Hector isn't already extinct, since she mostly feeds him little chunks of lint-covered Heath bars and stale Oreos she keeps in her pocket.

Turtles says she's going to fight for animal rights when she grows up. She claims there are 70 million pet dogs and 74 million pet cats in the United States alone, and they all need to be set free. I don't think she understands that 144 million dogs and cats roaming the country looking for kibble would not be a good thing, but try telling that to Turtles.

We gobbled up our cinnamon rolls like we were in an eating contest. After we cleaned the plate with our sticky fingers, we pounded down the steps to the basement, where my pumpkin seedlings were lined up in neat rows, ready for planting. Marylee and I started the seeds a month ago, in early May, to get a jump on the growing season while there was still a threat of frost.

We worked fast to lug thirty peat pots up to the porch. Since I was already behind, I wanted to get my seedlings into the ground.

"We have a *plethora* of seedlings," Cami said, her hands on her hips, "and I'm in a *quandary* over which ones to plant first."

"Can't you practice in your head?" I asked.

"What did I say to *elicit* such a sense of *persecution*."

"School's out, remember?" I said, but I couldn't help smiling.

"Are you sure you got the right seeds this time?" Cami said, squatting down to inspect the seedlings.

"Don't remind me," I mumbled.

"Did you check the labels?"

"Stop *harassing* me." That was one of her words from yesterday.

Three years ago, when I was finally old enough to race, I planted miniature Australian Blues instead of Atlantic Giants. By the time I figured out my mistake, it was too late in the season to start new seedlings. I wish Cami would stop mentioning it. It's not like she's never made a mistake.

My pumpkin patch is a quarter acre. You need a lot of room to grow pumpkins, because each seedling shoots out a vine that can hit fifty feet without even trying. Before you know it, you've got a million vines crisscrossing under your feet like a bed of pale green snakes.

Since the ground is still frozen in February, I spent March and April getting the soil ready. Now I had ten mounds of dirt for planting. If Mother Nature was on my side, by mid-July, about seventy days since the seeds germinated in my basement, my vines would be dripping with flowers and ready for an army of bees to pollinate the buds.

Everyone has their own secret recipe for growing giant pumpkins. I happen to know Sam buries fish guts around each seedling, a kind of super-strength vitamin juice for pumpkins. His mom works at a fish processing plant and she brings the guts home in old milk cartons, which is disgusting to me but not to pumpkins.

I was sticking with my recipe.

If you want to grow a giant pumpkin, you practically need to be an agronomist. That's a fancy word for "dirt doctor." Turns out dirt is way more complicated than you'd think. Since we live near the lake, we have sandy soil, so I have to dump in lots of peat moss, buckets of coffee grounds to jack up the nitrogen, powdered seaweed to add copper and phosphorus, and molasses to smother everything in calcium and magnesium.

Getting the right balance is tricky. Too much nitrogen, and your pumpkins don't grow fast enough. Too much potassium, and your pumpkin can explode, spewing seeds like shrapnel. Too little potassium, and you end up with a bunch of orange runts.

We nestled one seedling into each mound. I didn't skimp on the fertilizer. That's a fancy name for "cow dung." You need a lot of cow dung to grow giant pumpkins. Cow dung is like pumpkin candy. Pumpkins can't get enough of it even though it comes out of the rear end of a cow.

As soon as we had all the seedlings planted, I gave each one a big gulp of water spiked with chopped seaweed and molasses. Over the next few weeks, I would see which seedlings shot vines across the dirt like rockets and which ones didn't. The slackers would get yanked out and turned into mulch.

When I looked up, Sam was coming down the hill.

Sam is tall and lanky, and he can run fast and jump high, which is why the basketball coach is always trying to get him to come out for the team, but every time he asks, Sam tells him it would cut into his "reading time" too much.

The sun glinted off his shaggy brown hair, which looks like he cuts it himself. Probably because he does.

He climbed over the fence that cut between our two farms.

"Did you figure out the stumper?" he asked, kneeling down to press the dirt around a bare seedling as he smiled up at me.

I didn't smile back. The days when his charm worked on me were over.

"So? Did you?" he pressed.

I tried to ignore him.

Yesterday, on the last day of school, while we were

all staring at the clock, counting down the last three minutes left in sixth grade, Ms. Bagshaw reached into her desk. I thought she was going to pull out a bag of leftover jelly beans, because during the year, she'd give you one jelly bean for a good answer and two jelly beans for a good question. Instead she pulled out a picture of a wrinkly old man with a halo of spiky white hair sticking straight up like he was just hit by lightning.

"This is Albert Einstein," she said, holding up the picture.

We all looked at each other. School was almost officially over. No one wanted to hear about Albert Einstein.

She told us Einstein was the most famous scientist in the whole world (which I knew), about how he couldn't talk until he was four (which I didn't know), and about how he came up with the most famous equation in the world ($E = mc^2$) when he was barely out of college.

That's when the crickets in the heating vent began to chirp.

Why were there crickets in the heating vents?

Because Sam loved a good prank.

His favorite pranks usually involved food. The "cream-filled" birthday cupcakes that had toothpaste inside. Candy apples that were really onions. Valentine's Day chocolates filled with chili paste that set your mouth on fire.

Pranks with insects was new.

Sam put the crickets in the heating vent at the beginning of the year, and they were still going. Crickets are good breeders. I know that because Sam and I used to raise them in third grade to feed his pet lizard.

"Over the summer, I want you to figure out what Albert Einstein was thinking about the day he died," Ms. Bagshaw said. "And don't bother looking on the internet. You won't find the answer. You need to use your imagination."

She stood in front of the whiteboard, where she'd written, *I cannot teach anybody anything; I can only make them think.*

She said if you didn't use your brain over the summer, you could turn into an idiot almost overnight and flunk seventh grade.

No one cared. We were tired of *thinking.*

When the bell rang, we exploded out of our seats and shot through the door, snorting and pawing like wild ponies. Racing toward freedom, sucking in the smell of summer, Einstein was the farthest thing from my mind.

This summer was about one thing and one thing only: beating Sam.

3

That night after dinner, I taped my brand-new growing calendar to the back of the kitchen door. It had a grid of little boxes where you wrote in your weekly measurements, and a table for figuring out your pumpkin's weight based on the circumference.

Last year, my race pumpkin was 164 inches around and 58 inches tall and weighed in at 996 pounds. I grew one even bigger the year before that, but after I forgot to put the shade cover up, the skin got sunburned, and a rib cracked open and pulp squished out.

The world record weight for a pumpkin is 2,624.6 pounds. Growing a giant pumpkin gets a lot harder once the seedlings are in the ground. That's when I declare war against all of Mother Nature's sneaky little soldiers: cucumber beetles, aphids, squash bugs, and mites. Not to mention chipmunks, deer, raccoons, squirrels, and moles. And then there's black rot and mildew.

A lot of things could go very, very wrong before I made it past the first hurdle: getting all the flower buds pollinated. And that was four weeks away. Until that pumpkin was in the water, ready to race, you didn't know who was going to win the war against Mother Nature.

I'd just finished taping up the calendar when a raspy voice wrapped in static came over the shortwave radio jammed between the toaster and the cookie jar.

Dad looked up from the sink where he was washing the dinner dishes. We both heard the dreaded f-word.

Frost.

"There must be a backdoor cold front rolling in from the east," Dad said.

I glared at him even though it wasn't his fault. When you live on a bay at the western tail of Lake Superior, the sky can lean down in the snap of a finger and blast your island with funnels of freezing air, leaving a sheet of frost behind that can wipe out an entire crop.

"Will you at least help me put the row covers on?"
I asked.

"You know the rule," he said, grinning.

As if I could ever forget that rule. If your mom or dad helps you grow your pumpkin, you can be disqualified from the race.

I hate that rule. My mom and dad love it.

I ran out the back door and trudged up the hill to my patch.

I spread newspaper and mulch around the base of each seedling before I put on the row covers, little plastic tents staked into the dirt to protect the plants from the wind and the cold.

Sam was doing the same thing at the top of the hill.

When I could barely see my hands in front of my face, Dad brought his truck around and beamed his headlights over the garden. While I worked, he sat in his truck singing Irish songs. Even though he's been in America since he was eighteen years old, his Irish accent is still there.

"When Irish hearts are happy,
All the world seems bright and gay,
And when Irish eyes are smiling,
Sure, they steal your heart away."

I'd heard my dad sing that song a million times, but tonight it sounded different. I'd always thought it was a happy song, but tonight it sounded sad. I wondered if he missed Ireland. His mom died when he was born, and he said his dad was never around. That's all Dad would say about his old life.

By the time I was done frost-proofing my seedlings, it was late. Mom and Marylee were already asleep.

Upstairs I pulled off my dirty clothes, dropped them in a pile on the floor in my bedroom, pulled on my pajamas, and flopped into bed without even brushing my teeth. My mom would never let me get away with that. Just as Dad kissed me good night and tucked my quilt up under my chin, the quiet night was sliced open.

"Honey? Declan!" Mom cried out.

My dad bolted out of my room. I threw my legs over the side of the bed and slid down the ladder. My feet hit the floor with a thud.

"What? What?" my sister mumbled, groggy and confused.

I found my mom standing in a puddle of water in the middle of the hallway, my dad cradling her giant belly.

"My water just broke," she said as Marylee stumbled into the hallway.

"Water can break?" Marylee said, rubbing her eyes.

"The baby's coming!" Mom said. "Call the ferry!"

"Where's the stork?" my sister asked, looking at me. "You said the stork was bringing the baby!"

I didn't have to explain the birds and the bees to a six-year-old, because my mom suddenly squealed, "Hurry! He's coming!"

"He's not due for three weeks!" Dad said.

"Tell him that!" Mom shot back. She was swaying from side to side, a giant bowling pin about to topple over.

My dad disappeared into their bedroom, where I could hear him calling Grandma and then the ferry. The ferry was the only way on and off the island. I was glad it wasn't the middle of winter, when the ice is so thick, you have to go to the mainland on a wind sled. It's fun when you're going to school, but probably not so fun when you're having a baby.

"Where's my baby blanket?" Mom yelled. "I can't go without my baby blanket."

Dad hustled back carrying the yellow crocheted blanket they used to bring my sister and me home from the hospital. Mom grabbed it, clutching it to her chest.

My dad wrapped his arm around my mom's waist

and helped her down the stairs. As Marylee and I trailed behind, I wondered what my new baby brother would look like.

Unless "he" turns out to be a "she."

The doctor said my mom was having a boy, but I'm living proof doctors can be wrong. They thought I was going to be a boy, so my mom and dad named me Billie before I was even born. When I turned out to be a girl, they had to think quick. All they could come up with was *Sinopa*, an Ojibwe name, and *Finola*, an Irish name. While they tried to decide, they kept calling me Billie, and the name stuck.

Outside, Dad helped Mom into our battered pickup truck. Rust holes bloomed like flowers along the fenders.

"Where is she? Where is she?" Dad said, staring down the hill toward the road.

I was the first to spot two tiny headlights in the distance.

Grandma finally screeched up in her old Jeep, the tattered canvas top flapping in the wind. She was dressed in her pajamas and the fluffy fleece robe I bought her last year with money from my honey sales. As she got out of the car, she grabbed her overnight bag. Her long white hair trailed behind her like the wispy cirrus clouds you see on a hot summer day out on the lake.

She walked over to the passenger side of the truck and reached in through the open window to cup my mom's face in her hands.

"*Baamaapii,*" she whispered softly.

That means "until later."

Grandma kissed Mom on each cheek as my dad slid behind the wheel. As he peeled out of the driveway, sending a messy spray of gravel shooting onto the grass, Grandma wrapped her arms around Marylee and me.

"The baby's coming early," she said. "He's impatient to meet you."

I was excited about the baby, but I was also a little nervous. What if he cried all the time? And I definitely didn't want to change his diaper.

As my dad's red taillights disappeared into the night, we saw the ferry headed for the dock to pick up my mom and whisk her to the hospital.

Grandma herded us back inside, where we trudged up the stairs, discussing whether the baby would look more like me or Marylee.

"Tomorrow you girls need to start working on your

jingle dresses for the powwow," Grandma said as she tucked us into bed.

Every year, Grandma made our dresses from buckskin that felt like velvet. My job was to sew on row after row of tiny metal cones between rows of brightly colored beading. All Marylee had to do was a pick stitch hem.

"Do we have to?" she said, even though she had the easier job.

"Yes," Grandma said. "You have to."

I loved powwows. I loved the smell of venison meat roasting over hot red coals. I would even sneak bites when Marylee wasn't around. I loved the taste of fry bread covered in a snowdrift of powdered sugar. I also loved running wild, dodging fiery bits of ash spewing from bonfires like shooting stars, but mostly I just loved the food. And this year, it was close by. We didn't even have to take the ferry to the mainland.

"Why do we have to go to so many powwows?" Marylee demanded.

"So we can tell the stories of our ancestors," Grandma said.

"But I already know all those stories," Marylee said.

"We tell our stories every year so we don't forget who we are."

"Grandma, I'm not going to forget who I am."

"People forget who they are all the time," she said. "Our stories help us remember."

At the door, Grandma flipped off the light and said, *"Gi zah gin."*

"I love you too," I said.

"Me three," Marylee added.

As soon as Grandma closed the door, Marylee whispered, "Billie, do you ever forget who you are?"

"Never," I said.

I knew exactly who I was.

I was a girl who was going to get her revenge.

JULY

4

It should've been a perfect July day.

The sun was shining, a sweet breeze was blowing in off the bay, and white clouds floated by, a cotton candy slideshow.

Joey was supposed to have been born today. July 2. But I guess he got his dates mixed up, because he was born three weeks early. Maybe it was for the best. If he'd been born today, he might have thought all the fireworks on the Fourth were for him.

My mom said he had colic.

Colic is when a baby starts out cute but then turns into a monster.

I peeked over the side of my bunk.

Marylee was awake.

Without a word, we slipped into our clothes, tiptoed

down the hall, and peeked into my mom and dad's room. They were dead asleep with Joey nestled between them, wrapped up like a little burrito in his baby blanket. For once, he wasn't crying.

In the kitchen, there were no Cheerios, no bananas, no raisin toast, and no butter for the raisin toast even if we'd had it, which we didn't. And definitely no freshly baked cinnamon rolls. Nothing for us to eat, but almost a dozen little bottles of Mom's breast milk, all lined up in a row in the refrigerator.

My mom used a breast pump that looked like something you'd find hooked up to a cow in a barn. You could look at the milk and know exactly what my mom had for dinner the night before. Greenish milk meant spinach. Reddish milk meant beets. Yellowy milk meant mangoes or papayas.

As Marylee and I scavenged for food, Joey started up again.

I heard Dad's feet hit the floor above my head. A second later, he thudded down the steps.

The crying grew louder and louder until Dad burst into the kitchen, holding Joey in his arms like a football. Mom was right behind him, struggling to close her flapping bathrobe. He grabbed one of Joey's bottles out of the fridge and slammed it into the microwave, then jabbed at the timer with the tip of his finger.

"Why can't YOU get his bottle once in a while?" Mom screeched.

"That's what I'm doing!"

"You're only doing it because I got mad at you!"

"So? I'm doing it, aren't I?"

"But you're being mean about it!"

Mom's hair was all tangled up like a nest only a crazy bird would build. She pressed her fingers against her eyes. When she opened them, they were filled with tears. She looked right through me like I wasn't even there, and as quickly as Mom and Dad had blown into the kitchen, they blew back out.

Marylee and I stared at each other in silence.

Just then, Cami and Turtles appeared at the back door.

"Is it safe to come in?" Cami asked, her forehead pressed against the screen door as she peered inside our kitchen. I nodded.

We could still hear my mom and dad fighting upstairs.

"If we yelled like that, we'd be grounded," Marylee said.

At least Joey had stopped crying. I passed out spoons, and we all dug into the peanut butter jar.

"Your house used to be fun," Turtles said.

"Now your mom and dad sound just like our mom and dad," Cami added.

Turtles offered Hector a swipe of peanut butter from the tip of her finger just as Joey started crying again.

"Does he ever stop?" Turtles asked.

"Only when he's sleeping or eating," I said. "Let's get outta here."

"Bees first?" Cami asked. "Or pumpkins?"

"Bees," I said.

We slipped out the screen door and jogged up the hill. As we passed the barn, I glanced over at my pumpkin patch. After only three weeks in the ground, my main vines were each around thirty feet long, with secondary vines shooting off in all directions.

I'd stayed up late the night before, crawling around on my hands and knees, burying chunks of the main vines in wet mud so new roots would sprout and suck up even more of the nutrients in the dirt to feed the flower buds, which were growing from the vines on skinny stalks. These were the male buds. Typical. Just like in the lunch line at school, boys always show up first.

My bee helmet was hanging on the gate where I'd left it. I slipped it on and tucked the veil into the top of my T-shirt. If a bee stings your eye, you can go blind, so I always wore the helmet.

I grabbed a bucket and the hose to make some bee grub. We'd had too much rain and not enough sun all spring. Without enough sun, flowers don't bloom. If flowers don't bloom, they don't make nectar, and if they don't make nectar, my bees starve to death. And it's not like the bees can go snack on ants, because they're vegetarians, like us.

Marylee scooped a pound and a half of sugar from the storage bin by the gate and dumped it into my bucket. Cami filled the bucket up with water while Turtles swirled the water around with her hand to mix it up. When I couldn't see the sugar anymore, I lugged the bucket over to a hive and dumped the syrup into the top feeder. A gaggle of hungry bees buzzed around my head.

We had six hives stuffed with more bees than I could count. Our hives were healthy, which was a miracle, because about ten years before, bees around the world had started dropping like flies. Some scientist figured out that pesticides were to blame. Those poor bees would leave their cozy hives in the morning to go spread pollen around the world so that flowers could bloom and vegetables would grow, but they never came home, because pesticides scrambled their bee brains.

I hated to think of those bees flying all over the world and never finding their way back home to their queen.

Just as I dumped the sugar water into the last hive, I looked up and saw Sam running down the hill toward us. He jumped over the fence, like a runner over a hurdle.

"Check your bug traps," he said as he ran up.

"I don't need your gardening advice."

"Billie," he said. "Just do it."

I usually checked my traps first thing each day, but today I'd started with my bees.

Without saying a word, Cami and I barreled around the side of the barn, our feet pounding the ground. We skidded to a stop at the far edge of the pumpkin patch where my traps were hanging from the poplars.

I grabbed one and peered inside.

There they were.

Cucumber beetles. Some were still alive, trying to pry their wings off the sticky lining.

I would know them anywhere, with their fat yellow bodies and the ugly black stripes running down their backs. Prison suits for bugs. I wished they were in prison and not in my pumpkin patch.

To get rid of cucumber beetles before they wipe out your entire crop, you have to inspect every single vine and every single leaf like your life depends on it. You have to peer into all the dirt cracks around each plant, where the larvae like to hide out, because each larva sac has hundreds of grubs waiting to be born, and those grubs love nothing more than munching on pumpkin roots. Once the roots are ruined, the pumpkins slowly die on the vine, waiting for food that never comes.

We ran to the barn and grabbed rubber gloves and tweezers from the tool bin.

Sam came, too.

"I don't need your help," I said.

"Stop being so stubborn," Sam said calmly.

"Stop being so annoying," I shot back.

"You could also say, 'Sam, stop being *vexatious*,'" Cami said.

"Stop being stubborn, and I'll stop being *vexatious*," Sam said, grinning.

I considered my options. Since you can't win a pumpkin race without a pumpkin, and Sam did cheat me out of my win last year, if he wanted to help me win this year, who was I to say no?

We spent all morning battling cucumber beetles. Armed with tweezers, we'd flick one bug at a time into a big bucket of water. My dad said it was a painless way to go to bug heaven. It didn't look painless, but it did look quick. I felt bad about drowning a bucket of helpless beetles, but I had no choice.

While I was stabbing and grabbing cucumber beetles left and right, Sam blathered on about Einstein, his new best friend.

"Who even is Einstein?" Marylee asked.

"The most famous scientist in the world," Sam said.

"Why's he so famous?" Turtles asked.

"Because he figured out how matter and energy interact across the universe," Sam said. He wasn't even showing off. That's how he talks.

In my entire life, I have never once asked myself "how matter and energy interact across the universe." Why would I? I'm twelve. My brain isn't even fully developed! That's what Ms. Bagshaw told our whole class during the section on puberty in Science and Health. She also mentioned that going through puberty can make your feet stink. Which is why I wash my feet really, really, really well every single night.

"I keep wondering how we got here," he said.

"Where?" Marylee said, confused.

"Here."

"Um, you walked across the meadow . . . and . . . we live here?" she said.

"Not *here*," he said. He opened his arms wide like a conductor in front of an orchestra. "*Here. This world. Our universe.* I can't stop thinking about the big bang theory."

"What bang?" Marylee said. "I didn't hear a bang."

"It was fourteen billion years ago, silly," he said, ruffling Marylee's hair as she giggled.

I didn't tell him that I was *not* thinking about the big bang theory, so he took it as an invitation to keep going.

"And right after the BANG, the universe expanded like crazy and the very first atoms showed up."

"But what made the BANG go BANG in the first place?" Marylee asked.

I was tired of his science lecture.

"Seriously?" I said, scoffing. "That's the whole theory? There was a BIG BOOM and the entire universe just appeared?"

"Well, it was like the kickoff in football," he said.

"If I were a scientist, I'm pretty sure I'd be able to come up with a better theory than that."

"I'm sure you could, Billie," he said, smiling.

The last thing we did was wash down all the vines and all the leaves with organic soap, which is *supposed* to kill off any beetles lucky enough to escape the tweezer massacre, but all the soap really does is get your hands super clean. We don't use pesticides, because we don't want to scramble a bunch of bee brains.

"When are we going to harvest the honey to sell on the Fourth?" Sam asked when we were done.

Sam was a good actor. Every year, he always got a part in the school play. Right then he was acting like everything was normal.

"We?" I said.

"We're partners," he said as he brushed dirt from his pants.

"We *were* partners," I told him. "Now we're just neighbors."

"Have it your way," Sam said, grinning. After a quick running start, he leaped over the fence, and floated through the air as if he had the hollow bones of a bird.

That night, sleep kept skittering away from me.

I looked over at my collection of first-place blue ribbons pinned to the bulletin board above my desk, lit by a slash of moonlight.

There was the one for best handwriting in kindergarten.

And the one for learning the most vocabulary words in second grade. And for memorizing the multiplication tables before everyone else in third grade.

For spelling *prowess* correctly at the fourth-grade spelling bee and for turning a lemon into a battery for the fifth-grade science fair.

That had actually been Sam's idea, but he'd said I could do it since he wanted to grow bacteria in a petri dish.

I hadn't bothered pinning up my red second-place ribbons. Second place is just the first-place loser.

From my top bunk, I could see across the meadow to Sam's house. His window was lit up, a tiny postage stamp of light. He probably had his face wedged into some Einstein book.

My hand grazed the flashlight I kept jammed between my mattress and the side of my bed. In the old days, I would use it to send Sam messages in Morse code. We would talk like that for hours, forming words with pulses of light flying back and forth across the meadow like shooting stars.

But all the words stopped after last summer.

5

The next day, I woke up before the sun.

The cold morning air nipped at my skin as I yanked up my raggedy cutoffs and pulled on my favorite tie-dyed T-shirt. As soon as I checked my vines, I'd head out to the lake. I'd promised Grandma a big bucket of walleyes for the morning rush at her diner, Biscuits & Bass.

While Grandma's famous for her buttermilk biscuits, she also makes pierogi, which are Polish dumplings, only instead of using mashed potatoes and cabbage, she stuffs them with fish and beetroot. They sell out fast to the fishermen who are her regular customers—not to mention all the city people who'd be in town the next day for July Fourth.

I tried to slip away without waking up my little

sister, but I forgot about the creaky board by the door.

"Where're you going?"

She sat up in bed, half-asleep. Her biggest fear in life was being left behind when I headed off somewhere.

She scrambled out of bed and yanked on her jeans. "I want to come."

"No, you don't."

She looked at me. "You diggin' for worms?"

I nodded.

She swallowed hard.

Last summer, I threw a big ol' slimy red wiggler at her, thinking she'd giggle and jump out of the way. Only, it got stuck in her hair, and before I could pluck it out, she went crazy, screaming and clawing at her head like it was on fire, accidentally turning that red wiggler into worm sushi.

I still felt bad about it. I was just glad she didn't have eyes in the back of her head so she couldn't see me picking worm bits out of her hair all that afternoon.

At least worms don't have much blood.

"You promise not to throw one at me this time?"

"Absolutely."

I grabbed a bucket and a bottle of shampoo, and then we slipped out of the house. Before we headed to the dock, I checked the traps. Not one cucumber beetle. I went up and down each row and double-checked all the vines and all the runners. No sign of any nasty little invaders.

"Billie!"

I looked across the meadow. Sam was watering his patch.

"Your nasturtiums are ready!" he yelled. "Want me to bring them over?"

"I can get them myself!"

Marylee waited while I ran over to the glassed-in nursery plunked right between our farms. I found the nasturtiums nestled between the peonies and the marigold seedlings and grabbed two trays.

Every year, Dad gave Sam's mom a wheel of our homemade cheddar cheese in exchange for the nasturtiums. I plant them between the pumpkin rows because bees love the nectar buried in their blossoms. They come for the nasturtiums, but they end up pollinating all my pumpkin buds so they'll turn into actual pumpkins.

It's like giving a kid ice cream before they do their homework, even though that never happens in the real world.

I left the seedlings in the shade for planting later. Then Marylee and I headed for the lake, running full tilt through fat tufts of purple chicory. In the summer, Mom would get all excited and dig up a big mess of chicory roots and make "poor man's coffee," which she used to drink when she was a teenager. She said she liked to drink it for a trip down memory lane.

I tasted it once. It was brown water pretending to be coffee. Not that I even drink coffee.

We cut through a stand of birch trees that spilled us out near the lake.

The water was as smooth as Jell-O, but everyone on Madeline Island knows you can't trust the weather.

My dad loved to spout weather sayings. "A rainbow in the morning gives you fair warning." "When the stars begin to huddle, the earth will soon become a puddle." "Birds flying low, expect a rain and a blow." He'd taught me to keep an eye on rainbows and stars and birds.

My grandma's diner is an old ice-fishing shack bolted to the end of the floating dock that pokes into the lake. The waves make it rock gently back and forth, which is why mostly fishermen eat there. Fishermen don't get seasick eating their runny over-easy eggs at the counter. I'd seen more than one tourist bolt from the counter and barf my grandma's prize-winning pancakes into the lake, which made the minnows hiding under the dock crazy happy.

Now the sky to the east had a tiny hint of light sneaking up on it. When we reached the dock, I could see Grandma through the steamy window, bent over the grill cooking a mountain of hash browns. In the summer, Grandma runs her diner. In the winter, she's an auctioneer. She went to a special school to learn to talk fast and "enunciate crisply." So all winter, she travels around the country auctioning off cows and pigs and horses and cars and rickety antiques. Sometimes she gets lonely, but mostly she loves it.

My boat was tied up halfway down the dock. It wasn't fancy. Just twelve feet long, made out of tinny aluminum with an old rebuilt outboard motor bolted onto the back. But it was mine.

We pulled on the ratty life jackets I kept stuffed under the seats, and headed out, skimming across smooth black water. As we zipped past the end of the dock, Grandma swiped her hand across the steamy window and waved.

I smiled and waved back.

"Hold on," I yelled to Marylee, my hair whipping around my face. The engine whined as we picked up speed, and we sliced neatly through little rippling waves. I cut sharply back toward shore and rammed my boat up onto the sandy beach as far as I could. I jumped onto the sand, grabbed the anchor line, and tied a slipknot around a waterlogged tree trunk washed up on the beach.

"You coming?" I asked, grabbing my bucket. I dunked it into the lake and filled it with slushy water.

Marylee shook her head and hunched her shoulders higher.

Walleyes love chomping on worms. Especially big, fat red wigglers. I clomped around until I found a thick bed of old, moldy leaves in the middle of a grove of sugar maples. I dropped to my knees and cleared away the wet leaves and the slimy slugs until I could see the dirt.

"Wake up, little guys," I whispered, squirting a long stream of shampoo into the bucket of water. I swished the water with my hand, stirring up a big mound of bubbles, before I dumped the soapy water over the dirt.

My dad says it used to be a lot harder to dig up

worm bait, but now the whole state of Wisconsin is stuffed with angleworms and red wigglers. The newspaper calls it an "alien invasion" because the worms are hogging the good dirt and choking off the plants in the woods. My dad blames the beer-drinking, trash-spewing weekend fishermen who buy night crawlers from vending machines in the city, then dump the leftovers into the woods after a day on the lake catching salmon they don't even eat.

I smiled as dozens of squiggly red wigglers and angry angleworms shot out of the ground like fleshy rockets. Grandma taught me this magic trick. She said worms hate baths, just like kids do, but the truth is, they don't want to suffocate to death in soapy water. So they wriggle to safety, not knowing that they're actually headed straight for the sharp end of a bait hook.

I scooped up dozens of slimy worms and tossed them into the bucket, along with a handful of dirt. Worms feel naked without dirt to hide in. Besides, the sight of a bunch of naked worms might make Marylee start crying, because she knew what was waiting for them out on the lake. One minute they were daydreaming in their cozy dirt beds, and the next minute they were dinner in the belly of a fish.

I jogged back, lugging my bait, and plopped the

bucket into the boat. The worms were trying to escape by crawling up the sides, but since worms don't have hands, that wasn't going very well.

"Billie." Marylee pointed at the worms, frowning. "They're scared."

"They have brains the size of a flea!" I said. "They don't even know what's happening!"

"Worms have ears, you know!" she said. "They can hear you!"

"Actually, red wigglers don't have ears," I said. "Or eyes. Or teeth. Or bones."

"They still know you're mean."

I pushed us off and hopped into the boat without getting my tennis shoes wet.

As the light from the east seeped across the sky, Marylee and I took off across the water. In the distance, I saw my secret fishing hole.

And I saw Sam.

In his boat.

Ready to fish.

I let the throttle out, and we skimmed across the water.

"What're you doing here?" I yelled as we raced up.

"What's it look like I'm doing?" he said. "Hi, Marylee."

"Hi, Sam," she said, smiling at him.

"This is *my* fishing hole," I snapped.

"It's a free world," he said as he threw out his line. He got a bite on his hook right away. I watched as he wrangled the big, fat brown trout twisting and twirling at the end of his line.

"Sam," Marylee said. "Did you figure it out? The stumper?"

"Not yet," he said.

I gave her a look. "Since when are you interested in Albert Einstein?"

"It's a free world," she said with a giggle. Right in front of her, I threaded a fat red wiggler onto my hook. She glared at me and then looked away.

"But I did find out what happened to him *after* he died," Sam said.

"Stop talking," I said as we drifted closer to Sam. "You're going to scare away the fish."

"*After* he died?" Marylee whispered loudly.

"Someone stole his brain. Sawed off the top of his skull and just scooped it out."

"Why?!" Marylee said.

"To figure out what made him so smart. They sliced his brain up and looked at it under a microscope."

"What did they see?" Marylee asked, covering her mouth in horror.

"You want to hear something weird?" Sam turned toward me.

"No."

"I want to hear," Marylee said.

I shot her another look.

"You're not the boss of me," she said, cocking her head with her hand on her hip.

Sam grinned at Marylee. "His brain was smaller than normal."

"Really?" Marylee said.

"Yeah. Except it had more glial cells."

"What's a—"

"They protect the neurons in your brain." I said. I only knew that because we studied the nervous system last year.

"I thought you weren't listening," he said.

I clamped my mouth shut.

"I hope no one ever tries to steal my brain." Marylee touched her head.

While he went on and on about how Einstein loved to ride his bike and sail his boat and play his violin, I stuck another wiggly worm onto my hook and tried to focus on fishing.

My trick for catching walleye is to throw my line out three times, pull it in slowly to wake the fish up and let them know I'm there, and then count to ten and throw it out a fourth time with a really fast retrieve. That means you wind up your line as fast as you can so that the walleye has to fight for his dinner.

Before he knows what's hit him, he's in your net, ready for gutting.

Pretty soon, I had seven nice-sized walleyes scooped up in my net.

Sam snagged my attention when he said, "Einstein said that if you could travel faster than the speed of light, you could go back in time."

If I could go back in time, I'd change what happened between Sam and me on the lake last summer. I'd win and he'd lose, and everything could go back to the way it was.

I did the math to see what my chances were.

According to Ms. Bagshaw, the speed of light is 186,282 miles per second, and the fastest a real person has ever traveled is about 7 miles per second, and that was on a spaceship returning from the moon.

So I was pretty sure I wouldn't be going back in time.

Which meant no matter how hard Sam tried, our friendship was as dead as the driftwood we used to pile up for bonfires down by the lake.

6

Marylee wanted to hunt for gold on our way back, so I made a quick stop at her favorite beach, where you can scoop up a handful of sand and find tiny flecks of garnet and topaz and gold. The gold is just plain old mica, but I didn't tell Marylee that.

When we got back to the dock, Sam's boat was tied up in front of Grandma's diner. As I came through the door, I saw Grandma counting out crisp dollar bills. Sam's bucket of trout was on the counter.

"Grandma, what are you doing?"

"Buying some fish."

"You said you wanted walleye." I walked up, my bucket hitting against my leg with each step.

"Did I?" she said, all innocent.

"Yeah," I said. "You did. You said walleye. Not trout. Those are trout."

"I think your grandma knows the difference between a walleye and a trout," Sam said pleasantly.

"I'm not talking to you," I said.

"Technically speaking"—Sam tilted his head—"telling me you're not talking to me is talking to me."

I ignored him. "You're *my* grandma, not his," I said, glaring at her. "*I* get your fish for the pierogi."

"I told you walleye," Grandma said. "I told Sam trout. You know what they say: variety is the spice of life."

Sam stuck his hands into his pockets and looked down at his shoes, all fake humble. I saw the edges of his lips curl up.

I banged my bucket onto the counter, then slammed the screen door on my way out.

When Marylee and I got home, no one was awake, even though the sun had been up for hours. Before Joey came, my dad would have been grating zucchini for zucchini pancakes and squeezing oranges for fresh orange juice while he sang off-key.

At least Joey wasn't crying.

Marylee flopped down on the living room couch while I jerked open the fridge and peered inside. I saw watery cottage cheese, two kinds of wrinkly sour pickles, three kinds of vinegar, slimy-looking moldy cheese, stale bread, and apples that were so bruised, they looked like they'd been in a fight.

That's when I heard footsteps padding down the stairs.

"Morning, honey," Dad said as he nestled Joey into his little sling seat on top of the kitchen table. "Can you give Joey his bottle?"

"No," I said.

"Thanks, sweetie." He disappeared back up the stairs.

I looked at Joey. He stared back at me.

I filled his bottle, then propped it up on his chest with a dish towel. He sucked noisily.

I dug deeper into the fridge, but I didn't find any hidden bonemeal. Just some sad-looking grapes that were well on their way to becoming raisins.

I looked over at Joey. His face was turning red and splotchy.

I slammed the fridge shut and ran to him. He smacked the bottle away with a jerk of his hand, and it skidded across the floor, leaving a milk trail on the linoleum.

He looked like he was holding his breath. His face was getting even redder.

"Dad? DAD!"

Marylee popped off the couch. She took one look at Joey and turned and pounded up the stairs.

"DAAADYYYYY! JOEY'S CHOKING!" she yelled.

I could feel my throat getting all tight, like when you're about to cry. Just as I leaned in to pick him up, a ribbon of slimy, warm milk shot out of Joey's mouth.

My face stopped it.

I wiped my eyes and rushed for the sink, then splashed cold water onto my face. I dried off with a dish towel that smelled like an old sponge, and I looked at Joey. Now that he'd cured his indigestion, he was as happy as could be.

"DAD!" I yelled.

"What!"

"Joey threw up!"

"Well, clean it up!"

I looked at what was dripping down the side of the table.

"THAT'S YOUR JOB!" But I grabbed a wad of paper towels and wiped up the milk.

"I'll be right there!" Dad yelled.

As soon as he came down the stairs, I threw the soggy paper towels into the trash and said, "I'm outta here."

"Where're you going?" Marylee said, her voice rising in a whine. "I want to come with you!"

"No, you don't." I headed for the door.

"Yes, I do."

"I'm going to help Cami with her chores." Marylee liked cleaning out llama stalls even less than she liked being left behind. She puckered up her lips, twisting them to one side, thinking. "Have fun," she said.

I slipped out the back door and took off running. I slid under the fence at the edge of our farm, scuttling on my elbows. Then I popped up and darted through drifts of milkweed, which were almost as tall as me, before running across the hot blacktop road that separated our farms.

I found Cami and Turtles in their barn, mucking out the llama stalls.

"Didn't we just do this?" I said, reaching for my shovel, which was leaning against the wall exactly where I'd left it two days earlier.

"News flash," Cami said. "Llamas eat a *prodigious* amount, which leads to a *colossal* amount of *waste*."

We shoveled pile after steaming pile of stinky llama "waste" into our rickety wheelbarrow. When we had a mountain of you-know-what, we wrangled the wheelbarrow out of the barn and headed up the hill. The front wheel was almost flat, so it was slow going up the long, gravelly driveway, across the blacktop, and over the bumpy snake of a trail zigzagging through the meadow. Turtles trailed behind us, feeding bits of Oreo cookies to Hector. She'd take a bite, then give him a bite.

We finally made it up to my pumpkin patch. We pulled on our work gloves, stiff and caked with mud, and spread the llama poop around each seedling. I tried not to breathe too deeply, because what comes out of the rear end of a llama doesn't smell like perfume.

As soon as we finished, Cami and Turtles headed home while I jogged over to the bee yard. As I rounded the side of the barn, I saw Sam walking down the hill, his hands stuffed in his pockets. This time, he didn't vault over the fence. He just slid between the slats, then jogged over, until we were face to face.

"I'm sorry about the fish," he said. "Your grandma asked me to bring her some. I didn't think it was a big deal."

He sounded like he meant it. But how could I trust him?

We turned at the same time, to stare out over the water.

"Are you going to harvest the honey today?" Sam asked.

"Yeah."

"I could help you pull out the frames."

Sam knew I could barely lift the frames when they were dripping with honey.

"I don't need your help."

"I know," he said. "Just trying to be a good neighbor."

"You'd be working for free, because I'm not sharing the money."

"Deal."

Sam couldn't pull on his bee helmet fast enough.

He grabbed the smoker from the side of the barn. It looked like a foot-tall stainless-steel thermos with a pointy tin hat. He stuffed it with old newspaper while I grabbed the matches. It took a few tries before I could get one lit and stick it into the smoker.

A flicker of flame spread to the crumpled newspaper. Sam pumped the miniature bellows bolted to the side of the smoker, which shot air in and fed the fire.

I slipped on my bee helmet and lifted the tops off the first two hives.

In one box, I spotted a worker bee doing a wild jig, wagging her rear end this way and that, to let all the other worker bees know exactly where the best nectar was.

Sam pumped the bellows into both hives, wafting smoke over the dancing bees. If you shoot smoke into a hive, bees fall into a trance and forget how to use their stingers. Like magic, the bees stopped moving.

I hated to think how upset my bees would feel when they woke up and realized all their liquid gold had been stolen.

"Did you know the ancient Egyptians believed your soul flew into a bee when you died?" he said.

"Going from a human being to a bee doesn't sound like an upgrade," I said.

Sam was curious about everything. And he loved sharing what he learned. Nearly every day, he'd bring me a piece of the world, wrapped up in a random fact.

I mean, he used to. In the old days.

We pulled on rubber gloves and started yanking

the wooden screens out of the hive boxes, each one dripping with bees. I gently brushed fat clumps of buzzing bees back into the hive, leaving the comb exposed, fat and thick with honey.

We pulled out the frames from the first two hives and lugged them to the barn. Inside, we sliced open the combs and stuck the frames into the extractor, which is like a giant salad spinner. Once we got the frames lined up like the spokes of a wheel, I flipped the switch. The metal drum started spinning faster and faster and faster.

While we watched tiny rivers of honey run down the sides of the extractor into the big tub below, Sam launched into a whole speech about the meaning of $E = mc^2$, Einstein's most famous equation. He explained that E stands for "energy" and m stands for "mass" and c stands for the speed of light, and how Einstein figured out that mass has energy, and energy contains mass, so they're kind of the same thing. And when mass travels superfast, it creates a lot of energy.

Whatever.

But I couldn't help listening.

After we gathered the honey, I flipped off the spinner and pulled out the frames. Sam started filling recycled jam jars with honey from the catch basin. After

I washed down the frames, I headed outside to put them back before we grabbed more frames from the other hives.

Out in the bright sun, the air was thick with bees.

"SAM!"

Sam came running out of the barn. He knew instantly what was happening. The rich smell of fresh honey clinging to a gentle breeze was an invitation to every bee on Madeline Island to come to a wild bee party. While the party might be wild, it's not fun, because the host hive will fight to the death to protect their honey. And once bees start robbing a hive, it can take days for everything to settle down.

Unless we could stop it.

We slapped on the hive covers while a dark swarm of bees swirled above our heads.

"This is your fault!" I yelled. "You didn't put the tops back on!"

"Neither did you!"

"When am I going to get it through my head that bad things happen when you're around?"

Even though the air was alive with buzzing bees, Sam ripped off his bee helmet and threw it onto the ground.

Our eyes locked.

I saw two dark pools of anger staring at me.

I turned away and watched the guard bees fighting at the entrance of the two hives we'd opened, trying to save their food. As the invaders shot out of the hive, they dipped in the air, their bodies fat and heavy with stolen honey.

I watched as they stole more and more of my liquid gold.

What did Sam have to be angry about?

He's the one who ruined our friendship.

7

I had half as much honey as last year, but it still took Cami, Turtles, Marylee, and me all morning to get it into jars the next day.

We had to strain the honey through a big metal sieve that kept getting clogged with bits of honey-comb. After the honey made it through the sieve, we warmed it up in a homemade hot box so it could squish through cloth strainers I'd gotten at the hardware store. Before we bottled the honey, we scraped foam off the top, which dissolves in your mouth like cotton candy and tastes like water.

Later that afternoon, we headed for the lake, the honey jars settled into cardboard boxes lined with newspaper.

When we got to the dock, I went slowly over the

old, warped boards so my jars wouldn't break. I came to a stop in front of Biscuits & Bass.

Grandma had already set up my so-called honey stand, a rickety old table with one leg shorter than the other three, and millions of dried-up fish scales stuck to the top like a shiny varnish.

Each honey jar was wrapped in brown burlap. We used homemade bee stickers on the lids for labels, and Marylee colored in all the wings. As a finishing touch, Marylee tied a purple ribbon around each jar, since the Wisconsin state flower is the wood violet and she wanted my honey sales to take advantage of our Wisconsin state pride. I taped a handwritten sign onto the table so that the wind wouldn't steal it: HONEY $5.

That's when Grandma poked her head out of the diner window.

"Hi, sweetie," she said, smiling.

"Are you making faworki?" I asked. Faworki is the Polish name for the crisp cake rings that look like bows you could wear in your hair.

"That's on my list. Where's Sam? You always sell the honey together."

"Not anymore."

"But it was his idea in the first place," she said.

"No, it wasn't." Even as the words shot out of my mouth, I knew they were a lie.

Grandma looked long and hard at me while Cami fidgeted and Turtles melted away to the end of the dock.

"From the day you were born, I have felt only *minawaanigwad*," she said.

I knew *minawaanigwad* meant "happiness," but she didn't sound happy.

"Today, I feel the *agajiwin* you should feel."

A funny feeling started in the middle of my chest, right by my heart.

It was shame.

Agajiwin.

But I had nothing to be ashamed of. Sam was the one who should have been ashamed, not me.

Grandma's words were still hanging in the air between us when Mayor Philby walked up.

"Hello, Ziggie," he said to Grandma, with a big smile above his foot-long white beard. I hardly ever saw him smile, which was a good thing, because his teeth reminded me of little yellow Chiclets.

"John," she said flatly. Mayor Philby had a crush on her, and she didn't want him to get his hopes up.

"You hear about that high school kid down in

Milwaukee who got in trouble for launching a porta-potty a hundred feet up in the air with sugar rockets?"

I knew about the flying porta-potty. Everyone in Wisconsin knew about it. It had landed on the roof of the local police station. I didn't want to think about what happens when a porta-potty lands on your roof.

"How're your pumpkins coming, Billie?" he asked.

"Fine," I said.

"Course, we're barely into July," he said. "A lot can go wrong between now and race day. Mr. Jenkins from up on the other side of the island told me a bunch of hungry moles and nasty mites spent the weekend snacking on his pumpkin vines. Lost half his crop."

My hand froze, and I stopped straightening the rows of honey jars.

I'd been so busy getting my honey ready to sell, I hadn't checked on my pumpkins. Mother Nature was famous for letting you think everything was right with the world, then bam! A bunch of moles and mites turned your garden into their playground.

I didn't want to get knocked out of the race before it had even begun.

Cami, Turtles, Marylee, and I were panting by the time we rounded the barn and zipped through the bee yard to my pumpkin patch.

From a distance, everything looked good. But you didn't know for sure until you got down in the dirt and looked closely.

I dropped to my knees and started flipping over leaves, looking for eggs. Cami, Marylee, and Turtles did the same thing a few rows over.

"You see any?" I asked.

"Not a one," Turtles said, checking the longest runner.

"We got lucky," Cami said.

"This time," I said, breathing a sigh of relief.

After checking for the squash bugs, we spent an hour putting sunshades over my fastest growers.

We were starving by the time we were done. When we went inside, Dad was pulling homemade pizzas out of the oven. We scrambled to the sink and washed our hands, then jammed in around the table. Turtles picked off a glob of cheese for Hector. Then she ate her pizza rolled up like a burrito, which she claimed was how Italian people ate pizza. She's never been to Italy, so I don't know how she would know that. While we ate, my dad made German potato salad for the picnic before the fireworks.

"Why are you making German potato salad when you're Irish?" I asked, reaching for another piece of pizza.

"The Irish know how to brew beer, but the Germans know how to make potato salad that doesn't taste like potatoes," he said.

"If you don't want potato salad to taste like potato salad, why make it in the first place? Why not skip the potato salad and just make chocolate chip cookies that taste like chocolate chip cookies?"

Dad just raised his eyebrows and winked at me.

After we finished our pizza, Dad handed out grape Popsicles from the freezer.

"Outside," he said.

We flew out of the kitchen and jogged up the hill to my tree house.

Well.

It wasn't a real tree house yet because we didn't have a roof or doors or windows, but we did have a floor and walls. We even had baseboards. My dad had promised he'd finish the tree house before Joey was born, but that hadn't happened. Obviously.

Gripping our Popsicles, we pounded up the wooden steps threaded around the trunk of the tree and up through the branches, brushing past the bluish-green pine needles dripping with reddish-brown cones. I shot inside the tree house and flung myself onto one of the beanbag chairs Cami's mom had made for us.

I settled back and bit off a chunk of Popsicle. A tiny river of grape juice slid down my chin.

All of a sudden, the skin on my calves started prickling, like someone was poking me with a hot sewing needle.

That's when I saw them.

Field ants. With their ugly reddish-black bodies and three weird eyeballs all clumped together in the middle of their bumpy heads.

They were crawling all over us. As we scrambled up, we frantically tried to brush them off, scraping our arms with our hands.

"Get out!" I yelled. "Get out! Get out!"

Tripping and stumbling over each other, we hurled ourselves down the steps and then raced down the hill, screaming at the top of our lungs. As we ran past the barn, my dad came shooting out of the house.

"What? What?"

"Ants!" I cried.

We huddled on the back porch, and Dad looked us over. Our arms and legs were covered with angry red bites. Dad swabbed us down with calamine lotion.

When he was done, we looked like we were covered in pink paint.

That's when I saw Sam headed up the road, lugging a big bag of fish bonemeal.

He veered off the road and came up our driveway.

"What happened?" he asked, frowning.

"Why are you here?" I cried out, scratching furiously. "No one wants you here!"

"Speak for yourself!" Cami snapped.

"Ants," Marylee said. "A million of them. In the tree house."

And she started crying big, blubbery tears she tried to scrape away with the back of her arm. Before I could move, Sam dropped the bag of fish bonemeal on the ground and put his arm around Marylee. She buried her head in his shoulder, choking back tears.

"I wonder what they're after," he said. "Field ants usually live in dirt."

I wasn't in the mood for Sam's random facts.

8

Later that afternoon, I tried not to scratch my arms and legs as I checked my vines. I'd covered my bites in cool compresses after Dad drowned me in calamine.

My pumpkin buds were now the size of jawbreakers. In another week, an army of buzzing bees would swoop into my patch. I couldn't wait to see them traipse from flower to flower, all six of their furry legs dripping with bright yellow pollen crumbs as they worked. My pumpkins couldn't start growing until those worker bees fertilized my buds. The sooner that happened, the more growing time the pumpkins would have before the harvest.

By the time I was finished inspecting and watering, the sun was headed down. I went upstairs to change for the fireworks. I grabbed my favorite cutoffs and a tie-dyed shirt I'd made that has a giant sun on the front.

Mom appeared in my doorway, gently bouncing Joey in her arms.

"You can't wear that."

"Why not?"

"You have to dance the polka with Sam."

"WHAT?!"

"Did you forget that you and Sam were crowned king and queen last year?"

I stared at her, and then I sagged against the wall.

We'd danced in the competition as a joke. When Sam dances, he looks like a human pogo stick bent on reaching outer space, except gravity keeps snatching him back to Earth. We laughed the entire time, but I guess the judges had the last laugh when they crowned us.

"I have to sell my honey."

"It's one song." She cocked her head, looking at me. "You have to pass the torch and crown the new king and queen."

Just then Joey started crying. "Are you hungry, sweetie?" she murmured.

As my mom disappeared into Joey's room, she called out, "You're dancing the polka with Sam."

I threw open the door to my closet and looked for my polka dress.

As I rooted around, I remembered how Sam had said that Einstein loved to ride his bike and sail his boat. I suddenly wanted to act like Einstein and get on my bike and ride to the other side of the island, where I could hide out and watch the red-throated loons until the polka was over.

Anything not to have to dance with Sam Harrington.

But I knew I didn't have a choice.

I found my dress squished underneath the old telescope. Shoving the telescope aside, I grabbed the dress and stuffed it into my knapsack. I wasn't putting that thing on one second before I had to. I threw my knapsack over my shoulder, ran down the stairs, and burst out the back door. The screen door slammed shut behind me.

I flew down the last steep slope to the lake, cutting

through the tall grass. Below, along the water, a trio of red-and-white-striped big-top tents had been thrown up side by side.

I could hear the polka band warming up in the middle tent with "In Heaven There Is No Beer."

When I was little, I hated the polka. I'm not even sure why. Maybe it was the instruments. Instead of guitars and pianos and cellos and flutes, polka bands are addicted to squeezeboxes. That's slang for concertinas. They're a relative of the accordion, only they're harder to play, with many buttons on each end. A squeezebox sounds like a pig with asthma.

If you live in Wisconsin, it's not good to hate polka, because Wisconsin is the polka capital of the world. It's our official state dance, and you have to learn it in kindergarten. It's more important than learning your ABCs.

"Billie! Come here!"

Cami waved at me from On-a-Stick, her uncle Bert's concession stand, which was plopped under a hawthorn tree just past the last big-top tent. Every summer, Uncle Bert came up with weird things to eat off a stick. Last year, he featured a hot dog sliced up into the shape of an octopus. Not his best idea, judging from the weak sales.

"I can't believe he's making me wear a hairnet," Cami said, touching her hair with one hand and smoothing down her spotless white apron with the other.

I wanted to say I couldn't believe I had to dance the polka with Sam, but I knew Cami was on his side, so I didn't say a word. All I needed was more *balderdash* from her.

"You want to try the latest?" she asked.

"What is it?"

"Fried butter."

"Will it kill me?"

"No one's died yet," she said.

She took a hunk of butter, jammed a skinny stick up the middle, dipped it into a vat of thick batter, and dropped it into the deep fryer. When she pulled it out a minute later, she dragged it through a bowl of creamy frosting, plopped it onto a paper plate, and stuck it under my nose.

"That does not look good."

"Try it," she said.

I chomped down, expecting a burst of gooey, hot butter to shoot into my mouth, but the butter had melted into the batter, so it was like biting into a big, fat juicy doughnut. They were calling it "fried butter," but it was really just a doughnut shaped like a hot dog.

Cami calls that "marketing." I'd call it stretching the truth, but I didn't, because I wanted another one.

"Not bad," I said with my mouth full.

"Look," Cami said. "You've got customers."

I glanced toward the dock, where a gaggle of people were lined up in front of my honey stand. I popped the last piece of fried butter into my mouth and ate it running along the water, my feet slapping at the pebbly sand.

My first customer pointed to my blended spring blossom honey and held out a twenty-dollar bill.

"Here you go," I said, handing him the change.

"I use your honey in my homemade granola." When he talked, his Adam's apple bounced up and down.

I put his honey into a brown lunch bag and said, "That sounds delicious."

"I eat it every day," he said, reaching for the bag.

"Thank you," I said. "I'll have more for you next year."

We smiled, and he left. The next customer was bald, and judging from his beet-red head, no one had ever told him about the magic of sunscreen.

In less than an hour, I sold thirty-six jars of honey, including all my dandelion honey and most of my black locust honey, which left me with just four jars.

My last customer had bright green eyes and faded

red hair overrun with gray peeking out from underneath his jaunty little cap. He smiled at me as he picked up a jar and held it up in the sun.

"Would you be having any samples for a weary traveler to try?" I could tell he was Irish; his voice sounded like my dad's, the notes of a song strung together in words.

"Certainly." I grabbed the little plastic sample cups from the box under the table and the little ice cream taster spoons I got for free from Jean's Creamery.

I handed him the first sample. "This honey is—"

He held up his hand. "Don't tell me."

He dipped the spoon into the little plastic cup. When he tasted it, he closed his eyes.

"Spicy aromas and fresh fruit flavors with a clean, minty finish," he said, slowly opening his eyes. "Your bees were feasting on basswood nectar in April and May."

"Beginner's luck," I said, surprised I was being so sassy with a complete stranger. But he didn't feel like a stranger. And he didn't seem to mind. I handed him another sample.

"Can't miss the anise," he said after another slow, careful taste.

"Guess three in a row, and you get a free jar."

I handed him the third sample. He tasted it. "That's so easy, it's not even fair."

"You don't know, do you?" I said, smiling.

"You think I don't know?" he said, smiling back.

"If you knew, I think you'd say."

He looked at me as if he was trying to decide what to do.

"Ah, you got me," he said. "I'll take a jar of the basswood honey." He dug deep into his front pocket and pulled out two kinds of money. It took him a second to figure out which bill to give me. I gave him his change and his honey.

"Good day to you, kind lady," he said, and he headed off.

Then he turned back and caught me watching him. "If you plant some alfalfa near that buckwheat, you'll get yourself a one-of-a-kind honey." He reached up and gave a quick tug on the tip of his cap.

Buckwheat was the third honey.

As he walked away, I heard the polka music start up in the main big top. I took a deep breath. I just needed to get through the dance, and then I'd never have to dance with Sam again.

I grabbed my tin money box and ran over to On-a-Stick, and Cami. I threw my money box under her counter and changed into my polka dress in the muggy storage closet in the back of the concession stand. I could barely get into it, since it was a year old.

Cami giggled when she saw me.

I had on my black velvet vest with red, blue, yellow, and green ribbons sewn up and down across the front, and a wrinkly white silk skirt with matching ribbons. Only, they weren't up and down; they were sideways. I looked like a human Whirly Pop.

The big top was packed, and the polka band was in full swing. I saw Mom and Dad sitting in the stands with Joey. I waved, and they waved back as the band launched into "Polka Dots and Moonbeams." A gaggle of dancers swirled past with heel-toe steps, half steps, full steps, and shuffle steps, hopping with knees high and elbows flapping like a chicken. All classic polka moves.

"The Laughing Polka" came next. All the lead singer did was laugh to the beat. Laughter is supposed to be contagious. His wasn't.

I felt Sam standing beside me before I saw him. It was like his presence changed the air around me.

"Hi."

He acted like he didn't even remember leaving the tops off the hives.

Maybe he didn't remember. But I did.

He was wearing a polka costume I'd never seen before. He had on oversized red, white, and blue checkered pants with suspenders, red knee socks, black velvet boots with red tassels on the back, a straw boater hat, and a frilly white shirt with puffy sleeves.

He looked comfortable, like he dressed this way all the time.

The music started up again. As we stepped onto the dance floor, the caller placed a flower wreath dripping with ribbons on my head. Sam got one made of green leaves.

Our crowns.

"Just follow my lead," Sam said.

My eyebrows shot up. "Follow your lead? You can barely dance."

"Ladies and gentlemen, please welcome Billie O'Brien and Sam Harrington to the dance floor! Madeline Island's junior polka king and queen! One last spin before they pass the torch!"

Sam lifted his head, squared his shoulders, and held out his hand like a real polka dancer. I had to take it.

"Let's give them a big round of applause!"

The crowd cheered as the band launched into "Kiss Me, I'm Polish" and Sam led me to the center of the dance floor. He spun me and turned me and promenaded me. As we stepped and shuffled, round and round the dance floor, I caught a glimpse of Sam's mom, smiling and clapping to the music, a few rows back from my mom and dad, who were doing the same thing.

I couldn't believe it. Where was the human pogo stick?

He smiled at me. I didn't smile back.

"I practiced all spring," he said, reading my mind the way he used to.

Finally, the song ended. Except the crowd wouldn't let us go.

"Kiss her, kiss her!"

A flush of red crept up Sam's neck.

"Just do it." I tilted my head up, knowing they wouldn't stop chanting until he did. He quickly brushed his lips against my left cheek. His warm breath smelled sweet, like fresh mint.

The crowd stomped and hooted as if we were Polish royalty.

The new king and queen came onto the dance floor

and bowed before us as we took the crowns from our heads and placed them onto theirs.

Sam gallantly led me off the dance floor. As I turned to wave to the cheering crowd, I dropped his arm. When I turned back, he was gone, swallowed up by the crush of people.

9

The next morning, a snappy breeze rolled up the meadow and through my window. As I lay in the warm cocoon of my quilt, still half-asleep, I thought of Sam twirling me around the dance floor, my hand in his, his other hand resting on my back.

A smile was starting to sprout on my face, from a seed I hadn't even known was there.

What was I smiling about?

He learned how to dance the polka, and now I'm supposed to forget what happened last summer?

I wiped that smile off my face and looked across the meadow.

I could see Sam's entire farm from my window, including the periodic table of elements we'd painted on the back of his barn two summers before. It looked like a giant crossword puzzle, only the letters didn't make words.

Even though we weren't supposed to learn about all the elements until ninth grade, I already knew a lot about them because of Sam.

He explained it this way:

"If our alphabet is a list of letters that make all the words in our language, think of the periodic table as a list of substances that make all the matter in the universe."

Sam told me the whole world is made up 118 elements and human beings are mostly made up of just six of them.

Hydrogen. Carbon. Nitrogen. Oxygen. Phosphorus. Calcium.

Now I was wondering why all the elements that made up me were dreaming about Sam Harrington.

I looked out over the bay. After I checked on my pumpkins, this would be a perfect day to go fishing out on the *gichigami*. *Gichigami* is Ojibwe for "great sea." That was what my ancestors had named Lake Superior because it had waves like the ocean.

I could also practice my rowing for the race, going faster and faster until my muscles were burning.

But today was the powwow.

I peered over my bunk. Marylee was still asleep.

I eased down the ladder and slipped on the shorts and T-shirt I'd dropped in a pile by the bed the night before. Once I was dressed, I squeezed sideways through the bedroom doorway so it wouldn't creak.

Dad was already up, making chocolate chip pancakes. I hadn't seen him with a spatula in his hand since Joey had been born.

"Hi, Daddy."

"Your favorite pancakes coming right up."

I grabbed a pancake right off the griddle just as Ricky Two Eagle blasted up our driveway in his truck.

Ricky liked to brag that he was the best exterminator on Madeline Island. He even had a plastic sign glued to the side of his truck that said so. Of course, he was also the *only* exterminator on the island.

As he bounded out of his truck, carrying his dented red metal toolbox, my dad and I stepped onto the back porch. I tossed my pancake from palm to palm to cool it down.

"Hey, Ricky," my dad said.

"I know! I know!" Ricky blurted out. "Field ants! They'll be gone by tomorrow!"

I liked his confidence.

I leaped off the porch and walked over to him as I ate my pancake in two big bites.

"Don't worry, little lady!" he said. "I'll get rid of these nasty pests for you in no time. And you'll be happy to know that I use all-natural ingredients."

He pumped my hand so hard, I felt like a bobble-head doll.

I walked him to the tree house. He went up the winding ladder before me, and I followed. At the top, he stood in the middle of the floor, rocking back and forth in his mud-caked work boots. At least, I hoped it was mud. He also raised pigs, so it was hard to say for sure.

"Well?" I said.

He stopped rocking and started scratching his head. He frowned, and a ridge of flesh popped up between his eyes. When he raised his eyebrows, the ridge would wiggle.

"You got a real problem here," he said.

No kidding, I thought, as an ocean of ants scurried around us.

"Hear that?" Ricky said, holding his hand up like a traffic cop.

Tick. Tick. Tick.

"You got field ants, but you also got deathwatch beetles," he said.

"Deathwatch?" I said. "That doesn't sound good."

"That's not a fake name. In the old days, people thought those beetles came around when someone was about to die. But that's just a bunch of silliness. That sound? That *tick . . . tick . . . tick*. That's their mating call."

Great. So even as those beetles were invading my tree house, they were trying to get girlfriends.

Ricky kneeled down and opened his toolbox. "Let me get to work here," he mumbled.

Ricky started mixing up his concoctions while I went to my patch. I walked up and down each row, careful not to crush the tangled green vines underfoot. No pesky intruders. So far, so good.

Right after I finished soaking the dirt around each pumpkin with water, my grandma's Jeep turned into our driveway. I slowed my steps as I walked toward her.

"Boozhoo," she said when I reached her. That was Ojibwe for "hello." She was dressed in her ceremonial robe, with a yoke made of tiny cowry shells and beading all the way down the front.

"Hi," I said.

She tried to give me a quick squeeze, but I wiggled away from her. She gave me a look, but I pretended not to see. I still felt bad about the fish.

She looked up the hill and saw Sam watering his patch.

"Sam!"

He looked up.

She waved for him to come over, so he turned off his hose and jogged down the hill. When he ran up, he smiled at me while Grandma reached into her bag and pulled out a white muslin shirt with quillwork embroidered all down the front. She'd hand-sewn dyed porcupine quills in a geometric pattern across the front. She tossed it to me.

"Give it to him."

I walked over and gave it to him. As I did, my hand brushed his, and I remembered how his hand felt when we danced the polka. Warm and dry, and a little rough, like fall leaves dried by the sun.

"That's a traditional Ojibwe shirt," she said. "I want you to be my guest at the powwow today."

I stared at her.

Sam looked at me. I crossed my arms and looked back at him. Grandma watched us.

"Thank you," he mumbled. I knew Sam would never be rude to my grandma.

Grandma smiled and went to grab another bag from her car.

"Have you figured out the stumper?" he asked.

"Would you stop bugging me about that stupid stumper already?"

He shrugged, turning away.

"Have you?" I asked. I couldn't resist.

Sam turned back, all excited. "No, but I did learn all about Einstein's theory of relativity. Besides $E = mc^2$, it's his most famous discovery. And he came up with it when he was only twenty-five years old. He figured out that space is curved. It's like if you drop a bowling ball onto a mattress. Earth is the bowling ball, and the mattress is space. The ball curves the mattress. Earth curves space. And when space is curved, it affects time. So he invented a thing called 'space-time.'"

"Space-time?" I said. "Really?"

"What, you don't believe Einstein?"

"Last time I checked, the space around me wasn't curved."

I went inside to get ready for the powwow.

Through the kitchen window, I saw Sam head up the hill, his new Ojibwe shirt in his hand.

"Hello, *ingozis*," Grandma said to my dad as she breezed through the kitchen door right behind me.

Ingozis means "my son" in Ojibwe. Maybe she

should've said *niningwan,* which means "my son-in-law." But she says my dad was the son she never had.

"Pancakes?" he asked as she pulled three jingle dresses from her bag. They were for Marylee, Cami, and Turtles. Even though Cami and Turtles didn't have any Ojibwe blood, powwows were for everyone, a time to celebrate our heritage with old friends and make new friends.

When the doorbell rang, Dad wiped his hands on a kitchen towel and went to see who it was. Most people we know walk up the driveway to the back door.

It was the silence that made me follow him.

The man in the cap who knew so much about honey stood in our doorway. He stared at my dad. My dad stared back. Mom came down the stairs, holding Joey, who was asleep, and Grandma wandered in from the kitchen.

"Hello, Declan," the stranger said quietly.

Dad stood there like he was seeing a ghost.

"What are you doing here?" he finally asked. Anger and sadness were having a knock-down, drag-out fight inside him. Anger was winning.

"Tabhair dom logh."

"Nuair a reonn ifreann os a chionn," Dad replied, using a language I'd never heard him speak.

"Declan . . . Son . . ."

Dad slammed the door in his face.

No one said a word.

Until Mom made the mistake of asking, "Declan, was that your father?"

"That man is not my father! That is just some stranger who thinks he has a place in my life! He will not spend one night in this house, and none of you—NONE OF YOU—are to talk to him or pay him any mind at all! Do you hear me?"

Joey woke up and started waving his tiny fists like a baby boxer.

"DO . . . YOU . . . HEAR . . . ME?" Dad yelled, jabbing his finger at me.

Marylee came down the stairs, dragging her favorite blankie. "Why is everyone yelling?"

"WE'RE NOT YELLING," Dad said, before storming out the back door.

We trailed behind and watched him stomp down the driveway. When he reached his truck, he climbed in, slammed the door, and drove off, his tires spitting gravel.

His dad-not-dad was leaning against the fence by the street.

My dad didn't even look at him.

10

After Dad's truck disappeared over the rise, I slowly walked down the driveway until I was face to face with my new grandpa. We stared at each other silently. I looked back at my mom. She was still standing on the back porch with Joey in her arms, both of them sandwiched between Marylee and Grandma. She opened her mouth to speak, then snapped it shut, like a fish gasping for air. Finally, she seemed to find her words.

"Please," she called out. "Come in."

But my grandpa just tipped his hat and said, "I'll not be comin' in until my son invites me himself. Good day, now."

"Wait," Grandma said as she came down the porch steps. "We're having a powwow tonight. Come. As my guest."

"No, no," he said, backing away. "I won't be intruding."

She walked down the driveway until she stood beside me. "Please. I insist."

A long look passed between them.

"As you wish," he said. "But only because it would be as rude as rude can be to refuse an invitation from the likes of you."

With that, he headed down the street.

All of a sudden, he looked back and winked at me. I winked back.

Dad said I couldn't talk to him. He didn't say anything about winking.

"Don't you have work to do?" Grandma locked her eyes on mine.

I love how when grown-ups fight, they get mad at kids, like it's our fault. I didn't get sassy back because that wouldn't go anywhere good. I just rolled my eyes at the sky.

I had to help make the fry bread for the powwow that night. I'd had the same job the year before. The tribe elders had said that it was the best fry bread they'd ever had, so I was "invited" to help make it again this year. When an Ojibwe elder invites you to do something, you don't say no.

I couldn't stop thinking about my newly discovered grandpa. I had so many questions. How come he'd never come to visit before? Why was my dad so mad at him? And why had he come now, after all these years?

As I rolled these questions around, I headed across the meadow.

There was a fire pit where we cooked the bread, at the edge of the tree line by the big field where we always had our powwow. My dad had already started the coals and dumped off a bushel of corn and the stone mortar and pestle.

Just as I was about to go hunt for kindling to build the fire, Cami walked up, loaded down with maple leaves, ash kindling, and sun-dried pine logs.

"You're welcome," she said, dumping the wood onto the ground.

I grabbed some kindling and threw it onto the fire.

"Are you a bit *taciturn* today?" she asked.

"No," I said. "Are you a bit *truculent*?"

We grinned at each other. "Thanks," I said.

Pretty soon the pine logs were blazing.

As we let the fire burn down to hot coals, we started shucking the corn.

Before long, the ground was covered in tendrils of corn silk.

I sliced the kernels off into the stone mortar. As I reached for the pestle, Cami grabbed it.

"You hate this part," she said, and she started mashing up the kernels. It was a hard job. You had to lean into it with your whole body to make the pale yellow mush. Pretty soon, she was sweating.

"So?" she said.

"So . . . what?"

"What was all the yelling about? We could hear it all the way down the hill."

"Turns out I have a grandpa," I said.

"From Ireland?"

"No. The North Pole." Then I said, "Sorry. Yes, Ireland."

"Isn't that a good thing?"

"We're not allowed to talk to him."

"That should be easy for you," Cami said.

"What's that supposed to mean?"

"You know what I mean."

"No. I don't."

"You're good at ignoring people."

"Like who?" I demanded.

"Really, Billie? Like Sam. People like Sam."

"He deserves it."

"What is wrong with you? Why're you still mad about that stupid race?"

"Because Sam cheated me out of my win, and then he lied about it!"

"It was last summer! That's like a million years ago! Maybe he cheated, maybe he didn't! You told me yourself you didn't *see* him hit you! It doesn't even seem like something Sam would do. And what if he did tell a lie!? It's not like you've never told a lie! Why can't you get over it already?"

"What am I supposed to do? Pretend it never happened?"

"Isn't it enough that he always let you win at everything else?"

"What are you talking about?"

"For being so smart, you sure can be dumb."

We stared at each other.

"Thanks for your help," I said. "I can finish up."

Without a word, she threw the pestle on the ground and left. She didn't say goodbye. I didn't, either.

As I watched her walk away, I realized I was shaking my head back and forth.

Sam never let me win at anything.

Ever.

As the sun sank and the lightning bugs came out, we all formed a giant circle around the drummers. As each dancer entered the circle, the drummers tapped their drums softly. Grandma introduced the dancers by their Ojibwe names while Turtles, Marylee, and I twirled in our jingle dresses, a thousand tiny bells joining together.

After the last dancer was introduced, the drums grew quiet and the tribe elders sang the prayer song. When it ended, Grandma read from the ceremonial birch bark we kept in the cabinet in our living room.

"Five hundred years ago, seven Ojibwe prophets told us to leave the salt water and find the place where food grew on fresh water," Grandma began. Hands joined and we all grew still and quiet.

"Our ancestors traveled far and wide until they came to *Mooingwanekaaning*, the Ojibwe name for Madeline Island. Here we found wild rice growing on water, just as the prophets promised."

The chirpy whistle of an orange-breasted robin and the cry of a blue jay cut through the air. My dad says robins and blue jays are the poets of the bird world.

"The Ojibwe settled here and raised the Three Sisters," Grandma said. Her voice wasn't loud, but it was a voice that people listened to. Even the birds seemed to quiet down.

"Maize. And squash. And beans. The Three Sisters grew together and fed the Ojibwe for hundreds of years. And they still feed us today.

"We take the offerings of Mother Earth. We take them with gratitude, love, and hope for a peaceful future.

"*Ondaas! Niwiisin.*"

That was Ojibwe for "Come! We are hungry."

There was a swirl of color as people headed toward a row of tables longer than a football field. We found Cami near the front of the line. As she pulled us in beside her, she looked at me and shrugged. I shrugged, too. This was how we apologized without words.

The tables sagged with fry bread and wild rice and squash and stink fish, which was as gross as it sounded, but grown-ups loved it. I took a giant scoop of Grandma's wojape, a thick pudding made from cooked berries all mashed up together.

We loaded up our plates and sat under the giant canopy of an old ironwood tree, eating until our bellies were stretched tight. Turtles put Hector right on her plate and let him eat some of her squash.

I didn't see my new grandpa. Or Sam. Not that I was looking for him.

When the sky was silky black, the wild dancing started around the giant bonfire in the middle of the field.

The drums throbbed and pulsed as the grass dancers began, their bodies swaying in buckskins dripping in feathers and silky fringe, war shirts covered in fancy beading. I loved watching the dancers twirl past, their bodies moving to the beat.

As the first dance came to an end, I saw Dad standing in the flickering shadows of the bonfire.

I thought he was looking at me, so I gave him a little wave. But he wasn't. I turned to see what he was looking at. My grandpa was standing by the edge of the field near the trees, but the light from the fire still found him. His eyes were locked on my dad.

They reminded me of the two betta fish Mom had bought me three years ago.

At the pet store, I picked out a big glass fishbowl to put them in and brought it to the counter, where my betta fish were waiting for me, each one in its own clear plastic bag. The man at the cash register looked at the fish. Then he looked at the fishbowl.

"If you put them in the same fishbowl, they'll kill each other," he said.

So I asked Mom if we could get a sweet puppy instead of killer fish, but she said no.

I bought two fishbowls.

When we got home, I put the fishbowls side by side on my dresser. Hour after hour, their fins waving in rhythm, my fish would stare at each other through the glass.

It wasn't a friendly stare.

That's what Dad and Grandpa were. Two betta fish.

I thought about Sam and all the time I'd spent being angry at him over the last year.

It started out small, a sliver of feeling hiding in a dark corner of my heart, and then, when I wasn't looking, it secretly traveled from my heart and wedged itself in the middle of my brain.

And I got used to it.

But deep down, I knew it wasn't good.

11

Ever since Grandpa showed up on our doorstep ten days ago, my dad avoided him, while I avoided Sam, and the days limped by.

This morning, as I sucked in the sweet smell of jasmine riding in on a chorus of cicadas through my window, I wondered what my new grandpa was doing. He'd been sleeping in the barn or by the grape arbor, under the stars, rolled up in a faded sleeping bag that looked like it wouldn't keep a flea warm.

Wrapped in my warm blankets, I got worried. What if he got tired of waiting for my dad to talk to him and turned around and went back to Ireland? I never knew my other grandpa. He died before I was born. I'd never had a grandpa till now.

Right then and there, I decided that even though *my*

dad wouldn't talk to *his* dad, it didn't mean I couldn't talk to *my* grandpa. Besides, Dad was out on the lake. I knew he wouldn't be home until after lunch. What he didn't know couldn't get me in trouble.

I threw back my covers and skittered down the ladder from the top bunk. Marylee was snoring so loudly, the bed was practically vibrating.

I went downstairs and hit the button on the coffeemaker. As soon as the coffee was ready, I poured a big cup, with two heaping spoonfuls of my elderberry honey and plenty of fresh cream. That was the way my dad liked it, so I figured my grandpa might like it that way, too.

Outside, the cold, wet, dewy grass licked my feet, and the steaming mug of hot coffee warmed my hands as I walked up the hill toward the barn.

I found Grandpa burrowed deep in his sleeping bag under the tallest spruce tree on our farm. I knew it was a spruce because we'd learned about trees in Science last year.

I set the coffee mug on the ground nearby, plopped myself down on an old milking bucket, and waited. When he peeked out of his sleeping bag and saw me, he smiled and rubbed his face.

"Well, isn't this the most lovely way to start the

day," he said as he rose onto his elbow. He looked at the coffee. "Is that for me? Don't be teasing an old man."

He picked up the cup and took a long, slow sip.

"Why is my dad so mad at you?" I asked.

He took another slow sip before he answered.

"Who doesn't love a girl who gets right to the heart of the matter?"

"You didn't answer the question."

"I imagine he'll be telling you when he's ready."

"Well, I'm twelve, and he hasn't told me yet."

Grandpa climbed out of his sleeping bag. He was wearing jeans and a wrinkled flannel shirt. He stretched and looked around our farm.

"Just look at all the tree fruit that's come out to say hello," Grandpa said. "You've got walnuts waving and wild plums falling and meadow rue flowers winking at us like eye candy."

"How do you know so much about nature?" I asked.

"I can't even count the times I have walked from one end of Ireland to the other," Grandpa said.

"Don't they have cars in Ireland?"

"They have cars," Grandpa said. "For those who can afford them."

I asked my new grandpa what he did in Ireland.

"I'm a *seanchai*," he said.

"A shawn-who?"

"A *seanchai*. That's Irish for 'storyteller.'"

"That's your job? Telling stories? Is that a real job? Where you get paid?"

"Thousands of years ago, Ireland was wild and lawless. A bunch of fierce clans ruled the land. Each clan had a chief, and each chief had a *seanchai* who kept track of the clan history with poems and songs that were passed down from generation to generation."

"Was your father a *seanchai*?"

"He was. And his father before him. And his father before that. And on and on back in time for centuries and centuries. I followed in their footsteps."

"Why didn't my dad follow in your footsteps?"

He didn't answer right away.

"I am a storyteller," he finally said. "And just like a cow needs to be milked, I need to tell stories. About my people and my country. It's in my blood and it's in my bones. But it's not an easy life, walking from town to town, sometimes being paid with potatoes and a pint, sometimes being paid with a smile, which is lovely, don't get me wrong, but it doesn't soothe the hunger that comes to live in your belly."

I tried to think of all the times I'd been hungry in

my life. Who was I kidding? Wanting two desserts doesn't count as being hungry.

"Your father wanted better for himself. There was nothing for him in Ireland."

"But you were there."

Grandpa sighed. "True enough. But I was a father in name only. Not in deed."

"What do you mean?"

"I wasn't a good father."

No wonder my dad never wanted to talk about his life before he came to America.

After Grandpa finished his coffee, he went to clean up in the outdoor shower beside the barn.

Just then, Ricky's truck turned into our driveway. By the time I jogged down the hill, he was waiting for me.

"It hurts me to say this, but I've used every trick I know, and I just don't know what else to do. I hate to see your daddy throw more good money after bad when I can't help you."

As I shifted from one foot to the other, Ricky gave me a rundown of his "abatement history." He'd used cream of tartar, cinnamon, garlic, chili pepper, paprika, and dried peppermint to get rid of the field ants. None of it worked. He even spread petroleum jelly around the base of the tree, but the ants thought it was a Fun Zone at an amusement park and kept on coming.

"And those pigeons!" Ricky said. "That was a first!"

A posse of pigeons had shown up after the ants, with their special calling card: white poop. It's white because birds don't pee. Well, they pee, but their pee mixes with their poop and somehow turns it into white paste. Ricky told me it was from uric acid and that "back in the old days," people used to turn this stinky paste into gunpowder. The pigeons had a lot of fun spray-painting my tree house with their almost-gunpowder.

Hordes of chiggers and fleas and flies and lice had shown up with the pigeons. Ricky had hung fly traps and washed everything down with tea tree oil. None of it worked.

"This is my first real defeat in the animal kingdom, and I'll be honest with you. I'm taking it kinda hard."

"Well, thanks for trying, Ricky." I tried to be polite.

After he left, I headed over to my pumpkin patch, kicking at the dirt with the toe of my tennis shoe as I went.

I suddenly noticed the hum of buzzing bees.

My bees.

Flying right past my pumpkin patch. It was like watching a bee freeway with one exit ramp. And that exit ramp led straight up the hill to Sam's pumpkin patch.

This can't be happening, I thought, just as Grandpa rounded the corner of the barn, dressed and showered.

He took one look at my face and said, "What's wrong?"

"My bees aren't doing what they're supposed to be doing."

Grandpa looked around the garden, tracking the bees with his bright green eyes. He waded into my patch, carefully stepping over clumps of spiky red-and-yellow marigolds and raggedy clusters of peppers. I followed right behind him.

"What are you looking for?" I asked.

"I'll know when I find it."

I inched along slowly so I didn't crush any of the vines underfoot.

Grandpa stopped by the long, wiggly line of nasturtiums, which hadn't flowered yet. He kneeled down, pinched off a leaf, and peered at it.

"Here's your problem," he said, lifting up the leaf.

"What?" I said, confused.

"You planted chrysanthemums. Bees hate chrysanthemums."

"I planted nasturtiums," I said. "Bees love nasturtiums."

"If you planted nasturtiums, your bees wouldn't be feasting up the hill at your friend's patch."

"He's not my friend," I snapped as I took a closer look at the leaf Grandpa was holding. It was serrated, like a knife, only not with hard edges. More like ripples. Nasturtium leaves were shaped like lily pads.

Grandpa was right.

Those were chrysanthemums.

I whipped around and looked up the hill.

Cami and Sam were watering his pumpkins.

"REALLY, SAM?" I yelled.

Sam looked across the meadow. I reached down and started ripping the chrysanthemums out of the ground, flinging them through the air until it was raining dirt. When I looked up, Sam was running down the hill, Cami following.

At the bottom, he jumped over the fence and jogged toward me.

"What's wrong?"

"You were supposed to give me nasturtiums!"

"Billie—"

"BEES HATE CHRYSANTHEMUMS!"

"Billie, will you listen—"

"Shut up! Just SHUT UP! This is all your fault! You gave me the wrong flowers!"

"No! For once YOU shut up! I didn't give you the wrong flowers! You took the wrong ones!"

I realized he was right.

Which made me even madder.

"GO HOME," I yelled, right in his face. "I DON'T WANT YOU HERE!"

"Billie!" Cami snapped. "It's not his fault!"

Sam stared at me. He frowned, cocking his head to one side. Then he sucked in a deep breath and slowly let it out.

"You know what?" he yelled. "I give up. That's what you want, isn't it?"

"Yes! That's exactly what I want! Thanks for finally getting it!"

"Billie!" Cami said. "Stop being so mean!"

"Be quiet!" I glared at her.

"YOU be quiet!" she yelled, putting her hands on her hips.

"I thought I could get through to you, but I can't!" Sam said. "You're too stubborn! So guess what? I'm done trying to be your friend. It's like you said. We're just neighbors. And not the friendly kind! So you win!"

"No! You won! Remember? By cheating!"

He started to walk away, then turned back.

"By the way," he said, "I used your magic recipe on my pumpkins. Thanks for that."

"That's stealing!" I yelled.

"Really? I thought it was sharing. And sharing is caring. Didn't you learn that in kindergarten?"

He turned away and headed across the meadow.

"Everybody hates you!" I yelled at his retreating back.

"Everybody hasn't met me yet, Billie, so you're wrong again!"

"BILLIE!"

My head whipped around at the sound of my dad's voice. "Who are you to be talking to Sam like that?" He stood in the driveway, a bucket of trout in his hand. "That's not how we talk to our neighbors."

A hot bubble of anger climbed up my throat and shot out of my mouth. "Who are YOU to tell ME how to talk to people? YOUR OWN DAD CAME ALL THE WAY FROM IRELAND, AND YOU WON'T EVEN LOOK AT HIM."

"That's enough, young lady!"

"Billie," Grandpa said softly.

But I couldn't stop.

"He's been sleeping outside, waiting for you to look his way, and you tell me I'm not acting right? Well, you know what? WHY DON'T YOU GO LOOK IN THE MIRROR?"

"BILLIE! THAT'S ENOUGH!" My dad's face was flushed bright red. I didn't care.

I ran to the porch. As I jerked open the screen door, I saw Sam at the top of the hill. He sank to his knees, fell forward into the grass, and rolled over to stare up at the sky.

Why was everyone on Sam's side?

My sister. My dad. My grandma. Cami. Turtles. Everyone.

I went into the house and slammed the door as hard as I could.

That night, my dad made cauliflower mac 'n' cheese, one of my favorites, but I refused to eat. He pretended not to notice, because he was mad, too.

I slammed out of the kitchen as soon as the table

was cleared and went to my patch to pollinate my blossoms by hand.

One by one, as the sun sank down below the horizon, I peeled back the leaves on the boy blossoms, carefully pinched off the stamen, plunged it into the center of the girl flower, and rubbed it on the stigma, which looked like a tiny bowl of spaghetti.

I did what the bees were supposed to do. Only, instead of tracking pollen from flower to flower with hairy, spindly legs and clawed feet like a bee, I used my hands.

My sister was already asleep by the time I climbed into bed. My knees were rubbed raw from crawling around in the dirt all night.

As I nestled into my cool sheets and hiked my quilt up to my neck, I glanced through the window and across the meadow.

Sam's light was still on.

My eyes drifted up to the night sky and the Milky Way.

Ms. Bagshaw said there are over two hundred billion stars in our galaxy alone. She also said there's a black hole right smack in the middle of those stars.

I wished Sam would disappear into it.

AUGUST

12

Ever since our big fight two weeks ago, Dad and I still weren't talking. We were trapped in a fog stuffed with all the angry words we'd said.

Dad and my new grandpa were not doing much better. Grandpa kept trying to talk to Dad, and Dad just kept pushing him away. My dad was stubborn.

On top of that, it was August.

In August, it seems like all I do is work.

Starting with fishing.

The lake water is warmer in August. Well, to a fish, it's warmer. To a kid, it's still freezing cold. Fish don't like warm water, so Dad has to throw out long nets and troll along the bottom, where the water's cooler.

And even though Dad and I were mad at each other, I still had to help him.

I had to bait the hooks with dead smelt that smelled like rotten eggs and crank up the lines when we got lucky and snagged some wild trout. When you snag a razor-sharp hook through the mouth of a wild trout, he fights like crazy the whole way up.

After fishing, I helped Dad get his blue cheese ready to sell to all the big-city chefs who came for the Harvest Festival in October. My job was to blend in the mold that makes those wiggly blue veins.

I try not to think about people eating mold. It makes me gag. On the other hand, mold is also used to make penicillin, which saved Sam's life once when he got bronchitis so bad it turned into pneumonia and every time he took a breath, it sounded like two pieces of sandpaper rubbing together.

I guess there's good and bad in most things.

And every day there were my pumpkins.

My orange babies were packing on the pounds, sometimes adding thirty or forty pounds a day!

I had to get rid of all the pumpkin wannabes and make room for my best growers, since each main vine can only feed one giant pumpkin. If you want to top a thousand pounds, every single nutrient needs to go to that one pumpkin.

The first thing I did was pinch off all the pumpkins

from the secondary vines. Now those vines would send all their food to the main line.

I'd spent weeks walking around with my measuring tape draped around my neck, jotting down measurements to fill in the growing calendar taped to the kitchen door. I'd measure the circumference and plug that number into the weight table. I had some pumpkins taping out at a hundred inches around, which meant they were around three hundred pounds. I had some pumpkins pushing one hundred forty inches around, which meant they were over six hundred pounds.

So I was a pumpkin nanny.

Just like babies, my pumpkins had to be bottle-fed, only I did it with a big rubber hose. While they sucked up hundreds and hundreds of gallons of water every day, I had to keep them resting on a mound of dry sand and covered with sunshades. The fact that we were having a summer with record rainfall also helped my pumpkins pile on the pounds.

I saved the worst for last.

The llamas.

I don't like llamas.

Besides all the smelly spit, llamas are a ton of work. But Cami and I had a deal. She helps me with my pumpkins and I help her with her llamas. There's no way for me to wriggle out of it.

So every August, I help shear the llamas so Turtles and Marylee can spin the hair into yarn over the winter.

The word *shear* is very misleading. It sounds like something a made-up character in a fairy tale would do.

He sheared past the princess before he realized the danger he was in.

It was nothing like that.

Shearing a llama means wrangling a pair of electric clippers longer than my forearm and hoping the six-foot-tall, three-hundred-pound beast pawing the ground next to you will think that getting all his hair shaved off is a good idea.

And today was shearing day.

As soon as the sun was up, I headed down the meadow and across the road. I found Cami waiting for me outside the barn, dressed in muddy overalls. She was leaning on the paddock fence, her elbows planted on smooth rails that looked like the old gray bones of a skinny giant.

"Ready?" I asked.

"First we gotta catch 'em," she said quietly.

Even though Cami and I made up at the powwow,

we were still a little distant with each other. I wasn't going to change her mind, and she wasn't going to change mine, so we just avoided talking about it.

I looked at the pack of dirty, hairy llamas huddled in the far corner, waiting for us to make the first move as they stared us down. At least, I think they were staring at us. It was hard to tell because their beady little llama eyes were hidden under halos of stringy white hair. They could be Einstein's relatives, except they had four legs instead of two, and brains so small they could fit in a teacup.

Cami grabbed a long wooden pole with a hook at the end that reminded me of something you'd use at the circus to yank a clown off the stage. She handed me a grimy halter. "Remember. Divide and conquer."

We hopped over the fence. Cami went to the left, and I went to the right. The biggest llama let out an earsplitting bray, and they all started to hum to each other.

That was llama talk for "uh-oh."

At least they weren't spitting at us.

When we got too close, the whole pack stampeded. I froze and squeezed my eyes shut tight as eighty feet pounded past.

Well, they didn't really pound. More like they

padded past. Because llamas don't have hooves. They have toes. Two fat, leathery toes, just like a camel.

After a bunch of near misses, Cami got the hook around Jimmy.

Jimmy squealed like an angry pig and spit at me as I shimmied the halter over his soft muzzle and slipped it around his neck. After Jimmy, Cami quickly hooked Paco. Only because he stood still and let her. Probably because he was the littlest one in the pack. He knew his odds weren't good, so he gave up without a fight.

We led them into the barn, and I tied Jimmy up using a slipknot. If he went crazy and kushed, I didn't want him to strangle himself.

Kush is llama talk for "lie down."

Even though llamas have four legs, they only have two knees. So when they kush, they pop down on their front knees, then tilt back like a wobbly rocking horse and collapse to the ground.

You don't want to get tangled up with a llama when he kushes.

I looped the rope through the iron ring bolted to the wall and slowly pulled, forcing Jimmy's head higher so he couldn't get his head between his legs and start bucking.

After we got Paco and Jimmy tied up, we dumped

fresh alfalfa into the trough, a trick to keep them busy eating while we stole their fleece.

Cami handed me some clippers and a pair of leather gloves that were so stiff and old, I could barely shove my hands inside.

I turned the squeaky little knob to switch on my clippers. They vibrated hard, and I could feel my hands starting to tingle. Last year, my hands went numb halfway through the second llama.

I glanced at Cami.

She was making clean strokes across Paco's back, leaving a trail of soft stubble on top of bright pink skin. Mounds of fleece pooled around her feet like snowdrifts.

Paco actually looked like he was enjoying his rebirth as a sleek hairless creature.

When Cami saw me stalling, she flipped off her clippers and came over. Standing next to me, she parted Jimmy's thick hair at the bottom of his long, skinny neck.

"Do it," she said with a flick of her head.

I took a deep breath as I lifted the clippers and lined up the gnashing metal teeth along Jimmy's back. Even though I'd done this a bunch of times before, it always felt like it was the first time. I finally dug in, pushing into the wall of hair. Except I cut his skin instead of his hair. A thin line of bright red blood seeped out of a raggedy little wound.

Jimmy didn't even flinch.

"Wrong angle," Cami said calmly, pressing down on the cut with her gloved finger as she grabbed a tube of antibiotic cream. She squirted some cream on it and stopped the bleeding. But soon a long streak of red blood dripped down his side and dotted the cement floor.

"He's fine," Cami said. "Just keep going." She took my hand and gently positioned the clippers at the right angle. Before I knew it, I was knee deep in big, fluffy, snowy fleece balls.

That's when Jimmy let me know exactly how he felt about my clipper skills.

As I ran the clippers across his back and down his flank, I felt a stinging pain in my left buttock.

I yelped and dropped the clippers. They bucked around the floor, a mechanical fish gasping for air. Cami yanked the plug out of the socket and grabbed Jimmy's halter. Not that he was going anywhere. He'd already stuck his nose back in the alfalfa.

"What happened?" Cami asked.

"What's it look like? He bit me!"

"Let me see."

I carefully rolled down one side of my shorts and twisted my neck, but I couldn't see.

But she could. "Hmm."

"What?"

"Um, it's not that bad."

"Really?"

Jimmy lifted his head and looked right at me. It was like he tagged me last and we both knew it. I didn't know a llama could smirk. Cami told me, "You might want to put something on it."

I felt like I'd been quilled by a porcupine.

I left Cami to the llamas and headed up the meadow. As I trudged home, I saw Sam just ahead of me. He was looking up at the sky. When he turned his head, I caught a glimpse of his face.

He looked happy.

Sam was the last person in the world I wanted to see. I whipped around and headed down to the lake.

The dock was deserted. Even Grandma's diner was closed. I went to my boat slip, yanked the hitch knot off the dock cleats, and slowly climbed in my boat, where I sat down very carefully, even though the pain was melting away.

I shrugged on my life jacket and pushed off. As

I did, a wedge of yellow warblers swished past me, flying low and fast, their feathers the color of egg yolks, with faint streaks of red. Usually they hung out in the cottonwoods by the lake, since it was breeding season.

"Billie! Where're you off to, lass?"

Grandpa stood at the end of the dock, loaded down with two buckets of blackberries.

"Going to check my trap nets," I yelled back.

He set the buckets beside the diner door. "Would you be wantin' some company?"

The answer was no. I didn't want to talk to anyone.

"Come on, lassie!" he yelled. "Let me come along for the ride, won't you? I will let you have your thoughts in peace."

I turned the rudder and zipped back to the dock, where he climbed in and sat on the metal slat seat in front of me. He put on his life jacket and I gunned my little outboard motor, and we flew across the water.

I headed for a lonely pocket of water where I'd set up a system of buoys and mesh nets to trick whitefish into my trap.

The traps were empty. My traps were never empty.

We skirted around the buoys, and I found the problem. The net had a big dip in it. That's where the whitefish had made their way to freedom. I moved one of the buoys to get rid of their secret route.

My llama bite was still throbbing, but I didn't want to go in yet, so I let the boat drift.

I saw a rising mound of thunderclouds in the distance. Cumulonimbus clouds. We'd have to head back soon.

Grandpa pulled a bag of granola from his pocket, and we ate it all, lulled by the sound of the waves lapping the side of the boat.

"It's time," Grandpa said.

He said it so softly, I could barely hear him.

"Time for what?"

He reached over and took my hands in his.

"Time for me to go home."

I stared at him.

"Isn't this going to be your home now?"

"I have a home across the ocean, remember? In Ireland."

"But *we're* here, and we're your *family*."

Grandpa rocked back as my words landed on him.

"Why did you even come if you're just going to leave?" I said, starting to cry.

He reached up and tried to wipe away my tears, but I pushed his hand off.

"I wanted to help him find the strength to forgive me," he said.

"Why? So *you* won't feel so bad?"

"No, Billie. So *he* won't feel so bad."

"What's that supposed to mean?"

He sighed, his shoulders slumping.

"I wasn't a good father. That's no secret. I wasn't able to be there for him the way he needed me to be. I hurt him down to the marrow in his bones. But carrying that hurt around is like drinking poison and expecting the other person to die."

I felt like I was trying to figure out a really hard math problem, only the answer wasn't black-and-white.

"Every day, we make choices," he said. "We choose between love and hate. Between kindness and indifference. Between compassion and cruelty. Between anger and forgiveness."

Tears slowly filled his eyes.

"My own father left me to fend for myself, and I couldn't forgive him. It took me a long time to understand that when you choose to forgive, it frees you. But you have to choose it. It doesn't just happen. And until you choose it, you're trapped in the hurt."

I thought about Sam and me.

That's how I felt.

Trapped.

A distant crack of thunder boomed over the lake, startling us.

Now the clouds in the distance were the color of eggplants. I suddenly remembered the warblers swishing past me by the dock.

Birds flying low, expect rain and a blow.

"We best be getting back," Grandpa said.

I gunned the engine.

When the storm hit, it hit hard.

❧ 13 ❧

Freezing cold blasts of stinging rain slapped at my face.

"Billie!"

Grandpa's voice sounded tinny, a million miles away. But he was right in front of me, hunkered down on the metal seat, shoulders hunched, arms spread, each hand gripping one side of my bucking boat.

He twisted around to look at me. I kept my hand clamped on the slippery tiller and strained to hear him. The minute the words were out of his mouth, they were gobbled up by blasts of wind.

I opened the throttle all the way. The engine whined and wouldn't go any faster.

A long, low squall was headed right at us. In the

distance, I could see a waterspout spilling out from dark clouds down to the gray water below. It looked like a giant funnel.

The lake was starting to buck, the swells growing beneath us. The pelting rain turned into spitballs of hail. A jagged bolt of lightning cracked above my head.

For the first time in my life, I knew what real fear was.

I could see a sliver of land way in the distance. How did we get this far out? Then I realized we were caught in a rip current and it was yanking us away from shore.

A wave hit us out of nowhere.

One second I was gripping the tiller, and the next I was flying through the air until I hit the icy water.

The roar of the wind was gone.

All I could hear was the churning water rushing past my ears. It was almost peaceful. Until I saw Grandpa, sinking fast into the dark water. I swam toward him, kicking as hard as I could.

My lungs were about to burst as I stretched out both arms, fingers splayed, reaching, reaching, reaching until I just barely managed to grab a handful of Grandpa's shirt.

At last I figured out which way was up as I turned my face toward the murky light filtering down through the water.

Still kicking, I burst through to the surface. I gasped for air as a wave hit me in the face. Choking, gagging, it took all my strength to yank Grandpa above the water. He had a thin gash on his forehead. Bright red blood dripped down the side of his face to the corner of his mouth.

"Grandpa!" I screamed. "Grandpa!"

His head lolled.

I slapped him across the cheek. His blood stained my hand until the water washed it away. I slapped him again even harder, and he sputtered, coughing and spitting up water.

He looked around in a panic.

"The dinghy? Where's the dinghy?"

A giant wall of water crashed down onto us and shot us into a shallow wave trough.

I saw it.

My boat.

Upside down.

Again and again, we fought the surging swells of water as my boat played hide-and-seek between the waves. Grandpa gripped my arm so tight, I thought he might snap my bone in half, but I didn't want him to let go.

Over and over, we'd get close, then a wave would rise up and shoot us away. My arms got so heavy I could barely lift them out of the water. A crack of thunder ripped through the air, closer than ever as the biggest wave yet rose up.

Grandpa angled his body and faced the wave, pulling me with him.

"Get ready!" he yelled.

Just as the wall of water rose above us, he yelled "Now!" and dove into it. I took a deep breath and went right after him under the crashing wave. We popped up on the other side of the churning water. And there was my dinghy.

"Kick!" Grandpa yelled.

We kicked and kicked. Just when my legs wouldn't listen to me anymore, my hand landed on the cold metal of my boat.

After several tries, Grandpa managed to push me up onto the top of my turtled dinghy. I spread out and clung to the bottom.

There wasn't room for both of us, so Grandpa hung off the front end of the boat with his legs in the water and his hands gripping my shoulders.

We rode the waves as the storm raged around us. I kept waiting for the dinghy to roll onto its side and toss me back into the water, but every time we'd start to tip over, Grandpa would throw his weight to the other side and steady us. My teeth were chattering, and my lips were so cold I couldn't move them to make words.

The hail was coming at us from all directions, clawing at my face. Lightning and thunder flashed and boomed together.

We were going to die.

I looked at Grandpa. He knew what I was thinking, because he was thinking the same thing. He held on to me even tighter.

Freezing cold water washed over us again and again. It wouldn't take long to die in water this cold. After a while, I couldn't feel my hands. Or my feet. I wasn't shivering anymore.

I heard Grandpa yelling.

I was so tired, I could feel my dreams coming for me.

"Billie! Stay with me!"

But my dreams were stronger than his little voice, and pretty soon, I couldn't hear him anymore. Because

I was flying through the Milky Way on a beam of light. I couldn't believe how fast I was going. All around me, millions of stars shimmered.

When I came to the edge of the Milky Way, I saw one galaxy after another spreading out before my eyes. The name of each one was spelled out with banners made from flickering baby stars: Andromeda. Omega Centauri. Pinwheel. Sunflower. Tadpole.

Then I did what Einstein said was impossible.

I broke the laws of nature and began to fly through the universe faster than the speed of light. I was moving so fast I traveled back in time. Just like Einstein said would happen. And with each second, I could see the universe getting smaller and smaller. I went back fourteen billion years.

To the very beginning.

I watched as every single bit of matter in the entire universe was squeezed into a tiny point smaller than the littlest speck of dust.

And that tiny speck of dust exploded in the big bang, and I saw the birth of the universe right before my eyes. I was floating in the center of a giant firecracker as it exploded into a riot of color. Red and orange and yellow and blue and purple spears of light shot every which way all around me. Protons and neutrons and electrons bashed into each other.

Millions of years passed in an instant, and I watched as particles formed atoms and atoms came together and the universe gave birth to trillions of stars and planets and quasars and supernovas and comets and asteroids and black holes and nebulas and meteors.

And then I saw the birth of the Milky Way, our very own galaxy. Our sun exploded to life right before my eyes, and a gaggle of planets spewed out. Mercury, Venus, Earth, Mars, Jupiter, Saturn, Uranus, and Neptune began to spin around the sun, and the Milky Way took a bow.

A foghorn blasted away my dream.

Men yelling.

A big round spotlight swept over the churning water. More yelling. I was too weak to lift my head.

A pair of big, strong hands grabbed me and lifted me up.

A voice said, "I can't find a pulse on the old guy."

And I was sucked into a black hole in the middle of the universe.

14

I didn't die.

Grandpa didn't, either, but that's not the same as saying he was all the way alive.

The doctors were afraid he still might die from hypothermia. Hypothermia is when you get so cold, all your organs forget how to act. Like your heart forgets it needs to keep beating to keep you alive. Grandpa's heart was beating every once in a while, instead of nice and steady.

When the coast guard brought us to the hospital, the nurses wrapped me in heated blankets and hooked me up to an IV. I could feel my body warming up from the inside out.

At first, I was in the intensive care unit, in a room

with glass walls. I was surrounded by beeping machines and color monitors and IV poles and silver carts packed with bandages and gauze and tape and needles.

Mom was standing by my bed and holding my hand when I saw Dad through the glass as he ran up to the nurses' station outside my room.

"Daddy's here," I whispered. Mom squeezed my hand and walked out to him.

She reached out and placed both her hands on Dad's cheeks. She said something, and his face crumpled. His shoulders were shaking like they did when he laughed. Only, he wasn't laughing.

He slowly sank to his knees. Mom patted his back and let his head rest against her belly as if this was the most normal thing in the world. Then she helped him up and led him into my room.

"Hi, Daddy," I said.

He just looked at me, squeezing my hand like he wanted to make sure I was really there.

Then he asked, "What were you thinking?" His words were hard, but his voice was soft. "You know better than to go out when the weather's changing."

"I know," I mumbled.

"Don't you ever, ever, ever do that again. Do you hear me?"

"I won't."

"You almost sent me to an early grave from worry."

"I'm sorry, Daddy."

He leaned over and kissed the top of my head.

I closed my eyes.

He smelled like sweat and salt and algae and garlic, from the bait oil he used. I reached up and touched his cheek. I could feel dried salt. Then he rubbed his nose against mine, like when I was a little kid.

"You're my little girl," he said, his eyes all shiny.

"Go see your dad," Mom said. "He's over there."

She pointed to a brightly lit room on the other side of the nurse's station where two doctors and two nurses were checking Grandpa's monitor. The nurse was sticking white plastic tabs on his thin, pale chest.

Dad kissed my forehead. Then he walked slowly past the nurses' station into Grandpa's room.

The doctors and nurses looked up but kept working as Dad stood at the head of the bed. He stood there for a long time. Then he reached over and put his hand on Grandpa's shoulder. He leaned over and began to whisper into Grandpa's ear.

Grandpa had a tube in his throat, and his eyes were closed and he was very, very still. I don't think he could hear whatever my dad was saying.

I fell asleep. When I woke up, my mom was sleeping in a chair right next to me, her hands clasped together next to her cheek, like she was praying. The only light came from the heart monitor quietly beeping next to my bed.

My heart hadn't forgotten how to beat. I reached out and touched her hair. Our eyes met.

"Hi, Mommy," I whispered.

She sat up and squeezed my hand. Tears pooled in her eyes, and I saw how deep and big and strong and forever her love for me was.

She reached over and brushed my hair from my face.

"Is Grandpa going to die?"

She didn't answer right away.

"I don't know," she said.

Before I knew it, my chest was heaving with sobs. Mom climbed into the bed with me and wrapped her arms around me. Snot was spewing out of my nose. I couldn't keep up with it, so Mom just kept handing me tissues until the room was quiet again.

We lay side by side for a long time, with my mom stroking my hair and her arms wrapped all the way around me like I was a baby.

It felt good.

"I could've died," I said.

"Yes," she said. "But you didn't."

"How did they know to look for us?"

"Sam called the coast guard."

"Sam?"

"He saw you headed down to the dock. When the weather changed, he got worried."

I started to cry again. Mom just held me a little tighter. I knew she wouldn't let me go until I was ready.

I got to go home the next day. The doctors told me a hundred times that I was "one lucky girl."

Grandpa wasn't as lucky as me, because he had to stay in the hospital a little longer. But the good news was that the doctors said his heart had finally remembered how to beat the right way without being hooked up to machines.

Kids weren't allowed in the ICU unless they were patients, so Marylee and I didn't get to visit him.

While Grandpa was in the hospital, my dad turned the pantry off the kitchen into a tiny bedroom. It was cozy, with bright yellow paint and a window overlooking the meadow.

Five days after I got home, the doctors said Grandpa could come home. Mom left early to go to the hospital to get him because Dad had to fish.

Dad didn't want me to go out on the water with him, so I spent the morning in my patch. My pumpkins weren't doing very well. They got drenched during the storm and probably sucked up too much water. And I lost two of my biggest contenders when their stems tore away from the vines.

That meant certain death.

It was all my fault.

I hadn't positioned the pumpkins correctly. And I had two badly sunburned pumpkins. Their sunshades had blown off during the night because I hadn't tied them down properly. I was just waiting for the cracks to show up. I'd gone from seven contenders to three. After almost a hundred days of growing, the odds were suddenly turning against me. Not great timing, since the growth cycle slowed down as the days got shorter and the nights got longer at the end of summer.

After I finished checking my vines for any sneak

attacks, I sat by the edge of the garden and waited for Mom and Grandpa. Across the meadow, Sam was sprawled in the hammock he'd tied up between two pine trees, his nose in a book. Probably about Einstein.

When I saw Mom's car turn onto our road, I hopped up and ran down the hill. By the time her wheels crunched to a stop in the gravel by the house, Marylee and I were standing on the porch next to Grandma, waving our homemade Irish flags.

It was Grandma's idea. We spent the night before cutting and sewing together strips of orange, white, and green cloth.

Just as Mom pulled to a stop, Dad's truck came chugging up the drive right behind hers. He'd been fishing all morning, because the trout were running.

Marylee rushed over to the car, and Grandma followed with Joey in her arms, but I held back. As Mom helped Grandpa out of the car, Dad climbed out of his truck. Grandpa looked so pale and skinny, you could practically see right through him. He hugged Marylee.

When his eyes found mine, I started to cry. I really hoped I wasn't turning into a giant crybaby.

Using a new wooden cane, Grandpa walked over to me, carefully planting each foot. When he reached me, he slowly leaned over so we were eye to eye.

"I'm—I'm glad you didn't die," I sputtered.

"Me too," Grandpa said.

I saw my dad shove his hands deep into his pockets.

"Daddy made you a room," Marylee said as she walked over to Grandpa. "You're lucky because it's the room closest to the cookie jar in the kitchen."

Grandpa looked at Dad. "Did he, now?"

Dad shrugged. "Been plannin' on it since the girls were babies."

"Come in," Mom said.

Dad turned and walked toward the door. "Are you coming?" he asked. Then he disappeared inside.

"That's good enough for now, don't you think?" Mom said. Grandpa looked at her and sighed, nodding.

As she led Grandpa inside, a flash of movement caught my eye. It was Sam, watering his garden.

We stared at each other across the meadow.

Until he turned away.

I took a deep breath. I knew I had to talk to him.

My heart was pounding as I slowly trudged up the hill. By the time I reached the top, Sam had finished watering and was sitting at his picnic table, poring over a pile of dog-eared science magazines next to a stack of Einstein books.

"Hey," I said.

He didn't look up.

"What're you reading?" I asked.

He stared down at the page so long that I wondered if he was going to talk at all.

"I just found out that the big bang only created hydrogen and helium," he said.

"And?" I said.

"You can't make a world from just two elements."

"I'm made of six elements, right?"

"Well, ninety-nine percent of you is made up of six elements. One percent of you is made of potassium, sodium, chlorine, magnesium, and sulfur."

"So where did the other elements come from?" I asked.

"Supernovas. They're like element factories."

From Ms. Bagshaw, I knew that a supernova was an exploding star.

"Does that mean we're all made of star dust?"

"Exactly."

The words we were saying reminded me of the old days, except they didn't sound playful anymore. He looked over, and our eyes met.

For as long as I could remember, Sam Harrington had one look that was just for me. He even had it when I was being mean to him.

That look was gone.

"Why are you here?" he asked.

Why was I there?

There it was again.

That trickle of *agajiwin*.

Shame.

I looked away. My eyes landed on the stack of Einstein books. "Have you figured out the stumper?"

He shrugged.

"I haven't even started the assignment," I said.

"Do you want to borrow one of my Einstein books?" he finally asked.

"Okay."

He grabbed one from the middle of the pile and handed it to me.

The silence stretched out longer and longer, but our eyes held.

"Thank you," I said.

"You're welcome."

"Not for the book," I said. "For saving my life."

"I knew what you meant," he said.

SEPTEMBER

15

When August gave way to September, the air was thick and muggy, which made the hot days seem even hotter. Time moved in slow motion, weighed down by the weather. When my dad started ranting about the threat of global warming, it was hard to listen, because I was usually busy avoiding dive-bombing mosquitoes trying to suck my blood.

Luckily, Mother Nature was on my side. After more than a hundred days of growing, my last three contenders were coming up on a thousand pounds each. But unlike the year before, I didn't hover over my pumpkins. I watered them and threw on some liquid fertilizer, but not much else.

Cami and Turtles would come to see me, but I'd send them away. Ever since I'd almost died out on the lake, I hadn't been in the mood for company. More and more, they'd just cut across the meadow and help Sam weed and water his patch, while I stuck close to home.

My world got very small.

Sometimes I'd lie in the hammock for hours and just watch the clouds drift by, occasionally cracking open the Einstein book I got from Sam. Now that the summer was almost over, I figured I'd better get the homework done.

So I started reading, trying to figure out what he was doing the day he died.

Einstein said if you want to know anything about anything, you have to learn everything about everything.

Like that's even possible.

But since he was the most famous scientist in the world and I wasn't, I kept reading.

I read about Euclid, the father of geometry, and Galileo, the father of science, and Isaac Newton, the father of physics.

What's with all the fathers? Aren't there any mothers of science?

Meanwhile, all Grandpa wanted was words. He ate like a bird, but he gobbled up words. And not just any words. Poems. And only poems written by some Irish guy named Yeats. I said I'd read to him. Which turned out to be a bad idea because ol' Willy B. Yeats wrote more than four hundred poems.

And I read all of them. More than once.

I read to Grandpa every morning and every afternoon, and after a while he suddenly started saying the words along with me and I realized he knew them all by heart.

"If you already know all the words, why am I reading them to you?"

"I like hearing your voice," he said. "And words feed the soul just as eggs and toast feed the body."

"I'll stick with eggs and toast," I said.

Speaking of food, all of a sudden Dad started cooking up a big Irish feast every night. Colcannon was my favorite, even though when he first told me what was in it, I said, "I'm not eating parsnips and cabbage and leeks and parsley all squished together with mushy, boiled potatoes."

Dad just smiled and said, "You'll be eatin' your words and my food soon enough."

He whipped it up without a recipe like he'd been making it his whole life, and forced me to try it. I couldn't shovel it into my mouth fast enough. Dad even cooked meat because he knew what Grandpa liked to eat. He made a bunch of recipes I'd never heard of, like shepherd's pie, and corned beef and cabbage, and Guinness pie. Marylee wouldn't eat any of it, but she didn't make a fuss when everyone else did. One day, Dad made blood pudding for breakfast. It looked like the batter for red velvet cupcakes. When he said it had real animal blood in it, Marylee and I almost gagged.

Grandpa loved Dad's cooking so much he began eating more like a pig. Pretty soon he was up and walking, without his cane. At first, he could barely make it to the picnic table by the barn. He'd hook his arm through mine and shuffle along, walking a little farther every day.

Grandma helped, too. She'd show up after work with some special herbal concoction for him. When Grandpa had a little cough, she made him a mint poultice for his chest. When his fever came back, she made him black willow tea. When the gash on his forehead was slow to heal, she mixed witch hazel and water together and dabbed it on the cut.

September couldn't decide if it wanted to be wet and rainy or hot and sticky. Either way, the pink slowly drifted back into Grandpa's cheeks.

Just days before the race, I crawled out of bed before the sun was up and headed downstairs. I wanted to take a shower, but if I turned on the water, our clanky pipes would wake everyone up, so I decided to take one outside. Everyone was still sound asleep, so I grabbed a pair of shorts and a T-shirt and pulled them on as I tiptoed down the hallway.

I peeked into Joey's room. I thought he was asleep, until I saw his fat little baby arm through the slats of his crib prison, jerking this way and that like he was conducting his own private orchestra.

When I peered into his crib, his eyes met mine and he smiled at me. It wasn't gas, and it wasn't a muscle twitch, and it wasn't teething pain, because he didn't have any teeth.

It was a real smile. Just for me.

When he cooed, he sounded like a white-throated sparrow, with four little silky warbles. I leaned over the crib and picked him up. I waited. He just kept smiling, so I carried him downstairs.

In the kitchen, I made him a bottle. I decided not to warm it up in the microwave, because I didn't want to make it too hot and burn his mouth. I held it while he sucked away, like a hungry little guppy. When I told him about the pumpkin race, he hung on my every word, his big hazel eyes tracking my every move. When he was finished, I carried him outside.

We walked up the hill and around the barn, where I laid Joey on the ground near the shower, wrapped in my towel. He lay on his back and kicked his legs like he was riding a bicycle, while I ripped off my nightgown and jumped under the nozzle. I turned the rusty knob, and a cold blast of water hit my body and made me shiver. I scrubbed myself with a stubby piece of soap that had a tiny bit of life left in it. Pretty soon, I smelled like jasmine.

When I cranked off the water, I realized I didn't have a towel, since I'd wrapped it around Joey. Usually there was a pile of faded towels in an old milk bucket by the shower, but today it was empty. I scooped him up in the towel and walked across the yard, covered in nothing but goose bumps, just as the sun peeked up over the lake.

All of a sudden, I stopped, stark naked under the basswood tree.

Sam once told me that human beings are stuffed with about thirty-seven trillion cells, and every cell contains about a hundred trillion atoms. And each atom contains electrons. And at that second, I swear I could feel them all spinning wildly, full of life.

My breath sounded loud in my ears, and I could hear my heart pounding. I waited and watched and listened.

I heard the trill of two purple martins before I spotted them high above my head, darting between the branches of our basswood tree.

I smelled the sweet scent of the black-eyed Susans, the clingy sweetness of the daylily, and the rich odor of the chicory that lined the edge of my pumpkin patch.

Everywhere I looked, there were swirls of color: the red of the scarlet bergamot, the purple of the bellflower, the orange of the blanket flower, the white of the crowfoot.

I looked around at the only world I'd ever known, a world I knew like the back of my hand, and I felt like I was seeing it for the first time.

How did all this happen?

Sam said Einstein first got interested in science when his dad gave him a compass.

His world was never the same.

Because Einstein couldn't figure out what made the

compass needle move. That's when he realized there must be two worlds.

There was the world he could see and the world he couldn't see. In the world he couldn't see, magical and mysterious things were happening that made the world he could see what it was. Einstein wanted to know how that invisible world worked.

I wondered if it was like that with people.

Could friendships be mysterious, too?

Take Sam and me.

There was the part I could see, but there must be a part I couldn't see. Otherwise, I wouldn't have stayed mad so long.

I wanted to figure that part out.

That's when I remembered I was standing naked in the middle of the backyard, and I ran back inside.

16

It was a perfect day for the annual Madeline Island Pumpkin Race. Bright and cold and clear, with warm sunshine bathing my world from ninety-two million miles away.

When I woke up that morning, Marylee was perched on the top of the ladder, staring at me.

"You're gonna win," she said, all excited. "I can feel it."

Last year, I'd counted down the days and minutes and seconds until I'd heard the crack of the starter pistol.

This year, I just wanted to get it over with.

I was surprised to find Cami and Turtles waiting on the back porch, since they'd been hanging out with Sam. Cami must've read my mind, because she winked at me and said, "You ready?"

I nodded.

She made friendship look so easy.

Outside, the grass glistened with silvery slivers of dew in the morning light. When we reached my patch, I walked over to my three pumpkins. They were all just under a thousand pounds. And none of them were too long or too round or too flattened out from lying on the ground. Which one should I choose? As I examined them, I caught a glimpse of Sam up the hill doing the same thing.

After nearly four months of battling Mother Nature, it was time to cut the vine and get my pumpkin ready. Cami and Turtles and Marylee watched solemnly as I inspected each pumpkin, walking around them, running my hand over the tough orange skin and the long vertical ribs. I tapped the first one. Then the second. Then the third. I held my cheek against each one as I tapped, listening for a solid, hollow sound. You don't want to race a soggy pumpkin.

I made my choice. I picked the biggest one, because the really big ones float better and capsize less.

I slowly leaned over and cut the thick, twisty vine of my pumpkin.

We were ready to gut it.

I looked toward the house and saw Dad and Grandpa

headed toward us. They had the same easy stride. They walked fast, but they didn't hurry. Dad disappeared into the barn to grab his electric saw.

"You ready?" Dad said, walking up. His eyes were still crinkly with sleep.

Holding on to a bucking saw to hack off the top of a giant pumpkin was a dangerous job, which was why it was the one exception to the "do it yourself" rule. Except, Dad still wanted me to do it, so he stuck close by to make sure that the electric saw didn't get the better of me.

First, he gave me a Sharpie pen. I drew a black line around the pumpkin, closer to the stem than the middle, like you would with a jack-o'-lantern for Halloween, just big enough for a kid to slip into. Then Dad made me put on plastic goggles that were so scratched up, it was like someone smeared Vaseline all over them.

I was ready.

Dad handed me the saw.

I tightened my grip and flipped the switch. With a high-pitched whine, the blade whirred to life. I lined it up and carefully pressed it against the hard orange skin of my Atlantic Giant. As little squirts of pumpkin pulp shot out, I followed the black line I'd drawn.

Marylee, Cami, and Turtles stood back and watched with their hands over their ears.

When I was done, I flipped the switch, yanked off my plastic goggles, and handed Dad the saw. My hands and fingers were all tingly from the vibrating blade.

"Remember," Dad said. "When you lift off the top, everyone work together." He was thinking of the time when we got off balance and dropped the top. It slid to the ground and cracked the side of the pumpkin.

Cami, Turtles, Marylee, and I lined up around the pumpkin. We all slithered our hands into the slice I'd made.

"All together," Dad said.

"One, two, and three," I said.

We tried to lift off the top of the pumpkin, but it didn't budge.

"It's too heavy," I said.

He just smiled and leaned against the fence, sipping his coffee.

"Try harder," he said. It took three tries, but we managed to drag off the top and dump it near the fence. Up the hill, Sam worked alone on his pumpkin, sawing off the top by hand.

Last year, Sam and I gutted our pumpkins together.

This year, Cami went to help Sam, while Turtles, Marylee, and I teamed up to scrape out the slimy innards of my pumpkin. Long, wet, stringy strands that never seemed to end. Working together, Dad and Grandpa filled up bucket after bucket of pumpkin spaghetti and dumped them behind the barn.

Next, we lined the hollowed-out inside with rough, brown burlap flour sacks, clamping them down with thumbtacks. You didn't want to be out on the water inside a slippery pumpkin, because you could turn into a slimy pinball really fast.

While we worked, Dad started humming the Irish songs I'd heard since I was little. After a while, Grandpa began to sing the words, his voice frail.

Finally, Dad started singing, too. As they sang, I saw a look pass between them.

I watched, and then I figured it out.

It was a kind of love.

Like a song on the radio turned really low, but not so low I couldn't hear it.

It was time to load up our pumpkin boat and take her down to the lake. A dozen giant pumpkins on flatbeds had already passed by our farm, headed that way.

Cami and I carefully slipped a nylon harness around my racing pumpkin—a giant sling with a metal hook at the top.

Dad came back with the tractor and the flatbed. He lined the flatbed up by the gate before he unhooked it from the back of the tractor. Then he edged the tractor closer. He'd taken off the bucket he used to move brush and till the soil, and replaced it with a giant hook bigger than the anchor on his fishing boat. When I glanced up the hill, I saw Sam and his mom getting ready to load his pumpkin, which looked bigger than mine. His mom was just hooking up their flatbed to their tractor.

"Stand back, guys," Dad yelled to Cami and Turtles and Marylee. I stood by the side of the pumpkin, holding up the hook attached to the nylon sling. When Dad got the tractor close enough, I grabbed the hook dangling from the tractor arm and guided it.

"A little closer," I yelled over the chugging motor.

He edged the tractor closer so I could slip the tractor hook onto the sling hook.

I gave him a thumbs-up and skipped over to Cami and Turtles and Marylee. All Dad had to do now was gently lift the pumpkin and load it onto the waiting flatbed. We held our breath as he slowly moved the gearshift and the arm lifted. The nylon straps grew tighter and tighter.

And then the pumpkin was off the ground, suspended in the air like a giant orange globe. Dad carefully put the tractor into reverse and angled it so he was lined up with the flatbed.

Just as Dad was about to lower my pumpkin onto the flatbed, I looked down to swat away the mosquito sucking blood from my arm.

That's when it happened.

Thunk.

The sound of a big punching bag landing hard on cement.

My head jerked up.

My pumpkin had cratered, crumpling in on itself with big, raggedy chunks.

We stared in silence.

"The rain did that one in," my dad said. "Too waterlogged."

A flash of movement caught my eye up the hill. It was Sam, staring across the meadow at my crumpled pumpkin.

It was the rain.

That's what Sam said to me last summer, out on the lake.

And just like last spring, we'd had a really rainy summer.

For the first time, I asked myself a question I should've asked a year ago.

What if Sam wasn't lying?

I hadn't actually seen him hit me. I just felt it. I was leaning forward, my eyes locked on the finish line, digging deep with my paddle.

That's when it happened.

Thunk.

What if my pumpkin broke apart all on its own?

What if Sam wasn't a cheater and a liar?

What if I was just a girl who was quick to blame and slow to forgive when things didn't go her way?

17

The shoreline spilling down to the lake was packed with people perched on plastic lawn chairs and sprawled on blankets. Unless you were in the hospital with some contagious disease or on your deathbed, every man, woman, and child on Madeline Island showed up for the annual pumpkin race.

Twenty-four giant pumpkins already bobbed in the lake, tethered to shore, ready to race. I saw Sam right away. He'd painted his pumpkin blue and gold, our school colors.

The only pumpkin missing was mine.

Grandma, Grandpa, and I waited by the water's edge, squinting against the sun, as we watched my dad's tractor chug down the road to the water, hauling my second-choice Atlantic Giant. It wasn't as big as the first one, but it had a nice oval shape, perfect for cutting through the water.

I saw Mayor Philby trudging over with his clipboard. As he walked, he yanked a red-and-white hanky out of his pocket to wipe away the beads of sweat dripping off the tip of his nose. He looked like a human ladybug, with his belly and spindly arms and legs, except you didn't want him in your garden like you do with a real ladybug.

When Grandma laughed at something Grandpa said, Mayor Philby looked over and scowled. But the scowl didn't hide the sadness I saw in his eyes. He wanted to make my grandma laugh, too. But he couldn't.

"I'm sorry," he said, "but we're going to have to start the race."

Funny how people can act mean when maybe they're just hurt.

"Her pumpkin is almost—" Grandma said.

"Rules are rules," Mayor Philby said, cutting her off.

"Ever heard of Brian Boru?" Grandpa asked, his eyes locked on Mayor Philby.

"Nope."

"He was the High King of Ireland. He drove a bunch of bloodthirsty Vikings into the sea—"

"Tell your story to someone who wants to hear it—"

"The blood of Brian Boru flows in my veins. So if you think I'm going to let you wreak havoc on the spirit of my granddaughter, who has never done you an ounce of harm in her entire life, you're greatly mistaken."

Grandpa never even raised his voice, but the mayor still looked like he was having a stroke. His lips were moving, but no sound came out.

"You have two minutes," he said. As he huffed off, he pulled the starter gun out of his belt and headed for the dock.

I turned, shading my eyes, and saw Dad backing the flatbed into the water. In forty seconds, my pumpkin floated freely. Cami, Turtles, and Marylee waded through the water, guiding her to our starting spot, like little human tugboats. I grabbed my kayak paddle, and Grandma and Grandpa lifted me into my pumpkin, where I slid into position.

BANG!

The shot from the starter gun echoed across the bay and through the woods. Our paddles slammed into the water, like a horde of pelicans all dive-bombing at once. I paddled as hard as I could. A slow burn climbed up my arms and spread to my shoulders. Cami and Turtles yelled from the shore.

"Harder! Harder!"

Easy for them to say.

I saw Sam ahead of me. He was wearing his dad's old life vest, so he looked bigger. His pumpkin cut easily through the water. He was working hard. There were eight racers ahead of me. Including Sam. Inch by sweaty, burning inch, my pumpkin pulled ahead.

Sam threw a look over his shoulder, smiled, and went faster, taunting me. I started to paddle harder and slowly closed the gap between us.

I made it around the buoy.

The halfway point.

Now we were blasting back to shore. The crowd was cheering like this was the Pumpkin Olympics. After a flurry of ferocious paddling, I drew alongside Sam.

Our eyes met.

And that's when I laughed.

I don't know where that laugh came from, but it felt like it had been waiting to come out for a long time.

Sam looked surprised. And then he laughed, too.

It was like the old days, when we laughed together all the time.

I stopped paddling.

"What're you doing?" he yelled.

"Just go!"

He stopped paddling. Racers splashed past us, a wild jumble of bobbing pumpkins.

"It's no fun without you," he said.

We stared at each other, breathing hard as the cheers from shore washed over us.

"Have you been letting me win all these years?" I asked.

He looked at me.

"No," he said.

"You're lying," I said quietly.

It seemed like he wanted to say something else, but then he just shrugged and slowly paddled back to shore.

As I followed, I thought of Einstein.

He said if you look deep into nature, you will understand everything better.

I guess that's a fancy way of saying "Go look in the mirror."

That night, after dinner, I sat on the porch with a pencil and a piece of paper to scribble on. Since Einstein was a scientist and math is the language of science,

I decided to apply some math to the physics of Sam and me.

We'd been friends practically since we were born.

That was twelve years.

If you multiply 12 by 365, that comes to 4,380 days. If you multiply 4,380 by 24 for the hours in a day, you get 105,120 hours. Then, if you multiply 105,120 by 60, the minutes in an hour, you get 6,307,200. If you figure we were asleep for half that time, you could say we'd been friends for over three million minutes. And last summer, because of what happened during *one* of those minutes, I gave up on our friendship without a fight.

And what happened during that one minute? A boy won a race. And a girl stopped talking to him because *she* wanted to win.

In the *relative* scheme of things, what I did was wrong.

And Sam was right.

I liked winning. People you don't even know cheer when you win. Winning gets your face in the paper and free ice cream. Winning makes you feel special. Other people think you're special.

But if I always had to be the one holding up the blue ribbon, what did that say about me? And what did it say about me that I threw away my best friend over a pumpkin race?

A friend who once read me *Winnie-the-Pooh* forty-two times in a row after I got my tonsils out?

A friend who had helped me with my math homework every single time I had asked since first grade.

A friend who always laughed at my "knock-knock" jokes, even when they weren't funny. And they were never funny.

A friend who told me I looked cute after I got braces in fifth grade.

A friend who was always, always, always there for me, even when I was mean.

Shouldn't there be room for other people to shine in my universe?

I mean, even stars take turns. In summer, Vega shines the brightest. In winter, Sirius shines the brightest.

As I asked myself these questions, I began to look in my own mirror.

And I didn't like what I saw.

❧ 18 ❧

The first day of seventh grade was not what I expected.

Not.

At.

All.

First of all, Mr. Vernon said he wanted to find out what we didn't know, so he made us take a pop quiz, which he promised was "just informational" and "didn't count."

If it didn't count, why did we have to take it?

I hunched over my paper at my brand-new desk. He had equations up on the board with mixed numbers and decimals. He had questions about means, like what is the mean of 11, 10, 7, 9, and 13. He wanted us to add and subtract fractions and mixed numbers with different denominators.

As soon as we finished, we passed our papers up to the front, and Mr. Vernon left the room without a word. We had just enough time to start whispering before he returned with Ms. Bagshaw trailing after him.

"So," Mr. Vernon said. "Who figured out the stumper?"

Thirty-eight eyeballs drifted around the room. No takers. You didn't need to be an Einstein to predict that.

Ms. Bagshaw looked down, her lips lightly pressed together, as she clasped her hands and raised them to her chest, like she was praying. She wasn't mad. Just really, really disappointed.

I pictured the quote she kept on the whiteboard. *I cannot teach anybody anything; I can only make them think.* I finally understood why she'd given us the stumper. She didn't care about the answer. She cared about making us see that learning about the world is like peeling back the layers of an onion. She knew that one question always leads to another question, and sometimes when you get to the answer, it can make you cry.

I hadn't wanted to do the Einstein homework. But I did it because Sam gave me the Einstein book.

And maybe I was secretly afraid I'd turn into an idiot if I didn't use my brain over the summer.

"Anyone?" asked Ms. Bagshaw.

Next thing I knew, my hand was in the air.

"Billie?"

My fingertips rested on the top of my desk as I tried to think fast.

"Albert Einstein was working on his *theory of everything* on the day he died."

A few bored eyeballs landed on my face.

Sam was staring out the window.

"You're probably wondering, What *exactly* is a *theory of everything*?" I said.

"I wasn't wondering," Jamie Denton mumbled under his breath.

"Einstein wanted to figure out how *everything* in the entire universe worked, with one simple equation less than an inch long."

I glanced at Ms. Bagshaw. She looked surprised.

"Einstein figured out how the world worked on the grandest scale. And he was *convinced* that the littlest things in the universe should act just like the biggest things. Only, they didn't. Atoms and electrons and neutrons don't act like planets and stars and galaxies. The world of atoms is mysterious and unpredictable and random and uncertain. And that drove Einstein crazy. He was *convinced* the laws of nature that ruled the world had to be predictable and understandable and reliable."

My classmates were actually starting to listen.

"I'm like Einstein. I don't like uncertainty. It's a little scary. But I also love that the world is unpredictable and random. Because that means things can change in an instant. Like me."

I took a deep breath.

"Last summer, I lost a pumpkin race, and I blamed my best friend."

In a single swoop, every single eyeball in the room landed on me.

Except for Sam's.

"He's the kind of best friend anyone would want."

I felt my eyes fill with tears, but what I had to say was more important than a few salty molecules of H_2O sliding down my cheeks.

I took another deep breath.

"I hope he can forgive me and give me another chance to be the kind of friend he's always been to me."

My face was burning hot.

"Thank you, Billie," said Ms. Bagshaw.

Sam kept staring out the window.

I really didn't think Sam would be waiting for me under the flagpole after school like he used to, but I was still hoping. When he wasn't there, I gulped down my disappointment.

So much for my grand gesture.

Marylee and I took the smallest ferry over to the island, which was good because it was the fastest, but it was also the bumpiest, which was bad because Marylee has a tendency to get seasick. It's never fun when someone throws up on you, so I made sure to stay out of her line of fire.

Pretty soon, the ferry pulled up to the dock and we headed home on foot. When we came up the last hill, I saw Sam across the meadow, painting a new square on the lopsided periodic table of elements on the back of his barn.

I got an idea.

Leaving Marylee behind, I ran up our driveway and blasted into the house. I could hear my mom in the living room singing to Joey. I took the stairs two at a time and shot into my bedroom, where I threw open the closet door and dug around until I found what I was looking for.

The telescope.

Just as I was about to head down the stairs, I walked over to my bulletin board and looked at all my blue ribbons. One by one, I took them down and laid them in a neat row on my desk. I opened my closet door again.

Standing on my tiptoes, I grabbed the old shoebox I'd jammed way in the back on the top shelf. When I opened it, I found my red ribbons.

One by one, I pinned my red ribbons to the bulletin board.

I scooped up the blue ribbons, put them in the box, and gently covered them with tissue paper before I put the box back in the closet.

Lugging the telescope, I headed across the meadow on the old deer path, wading through giant drifts of yellow goldenrod and ragweed, the wispy leaves tickling my bare legs.

When I made it to the top, I leaned the telescope against the picnic table and walked over to Sam. He was adding the finishing touches to a new square.

"What're you doing?" I asked.

"Painting."

"I can see that."

A silence sat between us, but it wasn't a heavy silence, like before a storm. It was the silence of early morning, when the day is full of possibility.

"Some scientists just discovered two new elements," he said.

"Real elements?" I asked.

That used to be one of our big debates. Was an element real if it only existed in a lab for half a second before it changed into something else?

"What do you want?" he said quietly.

"I want to talk to you," I said.

Sam sighed, then dropped the paintbrush into the bucket at his feet.

"I lied," he said, looking at me. "I caught a swell and I hit your pumpkin."

I almost couldn't believe it. He *had* cheated me out of my win.

I slowly walked over to the picnic table and sat down.

"Did you even try to miss me?"

"No," he said. "I mean, it happened really fast. Even if I'd tried not to, I probably would've hit you. But I didn't. Try, I mean."

He sat across from me.

The anger that had wedged itself in my brain since last summer began to bubble.

But then I looked at Sam.

I saw he had his own *agajiwin*.

His own shame.

He'd wanted to win. Just like I'd wanted to win.

"There's more," he said. "You know ants really like peanut butter, right?"

"Yeah?" I said. "So?"

"Have you ever wondered why you can't seem to get rid of those ants in your tree house?"

"Sam! What did you do?"

"I put peanut butter behind all the baseboards," he said quietly. "I got tired of you ignoring me. I kept thinking you'd figure it out and we could laugh about it."

"Do you know how many times we had the exterminator out here?" I demanded.

"I'll pay you back."

"Yeah," I said. "You will."

Our eyes locked.

"That might be your best prank yet," I finally said.

"You think?" He grinned, like he couldn't help himself.

"Definitely a top contender."

We kept looking at each other across the picnic table.

At first, I couldn't read his expression. Then his eyes began to change, and I saw it.

The look he used to have just for me.

I smiled at him. He smiled back.

"What's that for?" he said, looking at the telescope.

"Remember why you got it?"

"Yeah."

"Let's set it up tonight," I said. "Maybe we can see the universe expand."

Was that even possible?

Maybe we couldn't actually see it happen.

But right then, I could feel it.

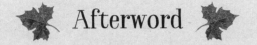 Afterword

Rob "Flashingbird" Goslin was an incredible guide through the world of the Ojibwe. Rob is an Ojibwe leader and a historian of the Red Cliff Reservation, which was established under the 1854 treaty with the Chippewa. As Rob explained to me, the Ojibwe refer to themselves as the Anishinaabeg people, which means "the original people." Madeline Island is sacred to the Anishinaabeg. They first arrived on the island around 1492, after a great migration that began five hundred years earlier, at the mouth of the St. Lawrence River in Canada. They were indeed searching for a place where "rice grows on water." While I am so happy and grateful that *The Pumpkin War* is now out in the world and in your hands, I will miss being immersed every day in this magical world.

Acknowledgments

"Thank you" is the best prayer that
anyone could say. I say that one a lot.
Thank you expresses extreme gratitude,
humility, understanding.
                                —Alice Walker

And so I truly and deeply thank . . .

Mollie Glick and Bruce Vinocur for believing in me.
For reading my manuscript in three days. For making
me do three rewrites. For selling it in three days.

Wendy Lamb for her editing pencil. And to the
amazing team at Random House I was lucky enough
to work with: Dana Carey, Colleen Fellingham, Alison Kolani, Bara MacNeill, Tamar Schwartz, and Bob
Bianchini. And to Jen Bricking, for her beautiful
cover.

Loch Gallagher, Tom Marine, Nadia Shields, Laura

Bickel, Merywynne Ruggirello, Sharon Lee, Laurie Anderson, Cecilia Falk, Kate Cushman, Pat Yahnke, and Tim Kusserow at Carlthorp School in Santa Monica, California, and Eric Mandel, Ken Asher, Camar Robinson, Kevin Kloeker, Daniel Koh, and Bruce Eskovitz at Windward School in Los Angeles for being incredible and inspiring educators who nurtured a deep love of learning in my children.

Dee Menzies for being an amazing elementary school principal and for giving my daughter the Alison Menzies Award, to honor girls everywhere who love to read.

Marcia Burkhart, Nicky Meyer, Sachi Hillson, and Sarah Defrance for being inspiring librarians who shared their passion for middle-grade books with my daughters and me!

Keldi Merton Leigh for sharing all your knowledge as director of the Madeline Island Museum. Whether the question involved the flowers, trees, geography, archeology, weather, or the history of Wisconsin, you always had the answer.

Lynda Lyday, Karen Gaul, Karin Aurino, Hilar Kaplan, Jean Pintarelli, and Millie Wilson for the laughter and the tears. And for being there. Just for being there.

Elizabeth Twaddell, Tana Reagan, Jennifer Small, and Terry Levy: you know why.

My fellow writers Jim Thomas, Marissa Moss, Shirin Bridges, John Sacret Young, John Wells, David Shore, Ali LeRoi, Hart Hanson, Justin Rubin, Holly Goldberg Sloan, David Hudgins, and Robin Swicord for hiring me, firing me, teaching me, and encouraging and inspiring me when I needed it most.

Karl Steinberg, Sandra Wolfson, Leslie Easton, and Deborah Steinberg for being my oldest friends. You are dear to me in ways you can't even imagine.

Bob Harrington, William Olvis, Alan Delameter, Frieda Ashendouek, and Jamie and Judy Dimon for your love and friendship.

Mary Sean Young and Donald Young III for being my sister and brother. Without you, this book wouldn't exist.

My mother, Lee Guthrie, for her fierce intellect and ambition.

My father, Donald Young, for always, always being proud of me.

About the Author

Like Billie, Cathleen Young grew up among story-tellers, and she often went fishing all around the Badger State with her father. After writing for magazines and newspapers, she moved into television. She has over a dozen television movies to her credit, including the award-winning *A Place for Annie*, which she wrote with her mother and mentor, Lee Guthrie. Young is now the executive director of HUMANITAS. She lives in Santa Monica, California, with her twin daughters, Gemma and Shaelee DeCarolis; her husband, Patrick DeCarolis; and Butch and Rexxy.

Visit Cathleen online at CathleenYoungBooks.com and on Twitter at @CathleenWrites.